MIDS

Dear

Michelle

Please, world

I can not be held

Responsible, for my mouse/

Many Blessings Mee

XX

First published by sistarsofthemoon publishing
London UK

Cover design from an original oil painting by
Jaqui Wells

Dedicated to my children Teresa and Tyron
With all my love

Set amongst the Cornish landscape rich in myths
and legends of the sea; a magical tale of romance,
intrigue and love

The soul of the soul of the universe is love
- Rumi -

PROLOGUE

She came to him from out of the sea – incandescent, pure in naked perfection. Even in this recurring dream, she was no stranger. She led him on a sensual journey to the turquoise depths of his subconscious. Her touch was emotive – intoxicating. They merged as one. His fertile mind was sinking in delirious euphoria. Then she was gone.

He found himself alone, sitting on top of the world, listening to the sound of the ocean call. Below, the landscape harmonised designs, weaving faultless patterns down to the shoreline. Through the soft summer morning, as if by magic, her lissom figure materialized, clothed in mellifluous black. She opened the rustic gate at the foot of the hill, the lush green fields stretching beyond.

Oblivious to the grating voice of the corncrake, she almost floated across the grass. Corn dollies dotted here and there glinted with the appearance of spun-gold thread. Sunlight touched her waterfall of dark hair, creating music from the innermost recesses of his mind, accompanied by haunting strains of an inspiring Gregorian chant. She epitomized light, lifting him to some enchanted realm. To speak would break the spell. 'Aphrodite – born of the sea – carried on the breeze – to steal thy soul.' The jumbled words slid across his mind, smooth as silk.

An odd premonition flickered through his thoughts. The salt spray of the sea crashed like cymbals against the Cornish cliffs, white foam breaking into tiny diamond particles. Music echoed. His instincts urged him to run after her, but his feet moved in slow motion. Barefoot, she ran on into the wind-whipped waves.

The shark, dodging the floats of the fishing trawler, its silvery finn gliding stealthily in her direction… Sharp fangs clamped together like the cold steel of a wild animal trap. The girl disappeared from his stimulated senses, the ocean extinguishing her glow.

"No!" His loud lament of anguish jarred the atmosphere, reverberating in his head.

"Wake up, wake up!" Somebody was shaking him.

"That must have been some nightmare Howard. You slept through the storm."

"What! What! Where am I?" He was disorientated, between that unreal state of sleeping and waking.

The ships clock struck twelve.

"You're aboard ship and we're about to dock at Amsterdam any minute," replied Hans.

Moments of relief mingled with regret, as he was forced to leave the girl of his dreams to her fate.

Chapter 1

Naida sat bolt upright as the train screeched to a halt. The gathering clouds hid the waning moon on this wet summer night of 83. With hindsight, she realised, it had been foolish to occupy the empty compartment. But in her haste to escape she had been careless. She looked out of the window at the deserted station. Rain lashed down onto the platform in huge droplets, making her shiver. She supposed it must be midnight by now.

Footsteps approached. Naida stiffened, willing them, with a force bordering on terror, to stop short of her carriage. A shuddering sigh racked her body as she heard them pause further along and then a door slammed. The train began to amble on, out into the black night. Her reaction had been more acute, owing to the reason for her journey. She was alone again in the carriage with nothing but the occasional rumble of far away thunder.

Three stops later, much to her relief, she changed trains and was aboard the high-speed inter-city, winging its way to Cornwall. Naida dozed spasmodically. Eventually the soft dawn light lit the countryside, alleviating her fears.

The sky was blue once more as she stepped down from the train. After enquiring about buses to Perranuthnoe, she finally reached the village and made straight for Old Moorstone Farm. It was easy to find from the little map her Mother had drawn and thrust into her hand that fateful night.

Naida approached the main lane leading to the farmhouse. An elderly man was seated outside. He pulled his hat down to shade his face from the sun. Then she saw him raise his eyes again and focus on her. She slowed down, apprehension crept over her. However, it would be foolish to turn back. Her rucksack was beginning to become a burden. With effort she forced herself to continue. Drawing closer, she eyed the old Cornishman with trepidation.

"Good morning," she ventured. "I'm looking for a Mr. Ivor Tregartha. I understand he lives here"

"Mornin'." The old man lit his pipe and leaned back in his chair. The girl looked strangely familiar. "Oh yes, that be right missy." He flicked the rim of his hat up again and gazed at her quizzically. " Ivor – he be at market. You're more than welcome to wait."

Naida tossed her dark hair away from her face, wishing she had tied it back. She was tired and longed for a quick shower after the hasty and hot journey. "How long will he be?" she enquired.

The old man squinted in the sun. "He be back soon. Got somewhere to stay? You'll not find any vacancies this time o' year you know. Was Ivor expecting
you?"

Naida looked down. Her heavy hair fell across her cheek again. "No, I was told back in London that I should call in to see Mr. Tregartha, as he lets out rooms." She was beginning to wonder what on earth had possessed her to come.

2

"Ah well there's no harm in the asking," he replied absently

By now Naida was mentally and physically exhausted. "Then I would like to wait for him, if you don't mind," she said and introduced herself. "I'm Naida Batis"

"Pleased to meet you Naida, they call me Old Tom," he said, easing himself out of his chair to shake her hand. "Take a seat."

Naida untangled herself from her rucksack and let it fall to the ground. Thankfully she sank down into the comfortable chair, while Tom went inside to bring another chair for himself. Naida was glad to be left alone for a minute and hoped to avoid any inquisitive questions the old man might be inclined to ask. Doubting her own motives uncertainties crowded her mind.

Tom returned with two cool drinks. "You look like you could do with this," He said, handing her a tall glass.

"Thank you." She marvelled at his hospitality.

He set his chair down beside hers, obviously pleased to have some company. "Hear the storm last night?"

"It rained heavily on the journey," she answered. "I heard the thunder."
He sipped his drink slowly. "I was just sitting 'ere this morning, my thoughts with the fishermen. I've known many a long day across the channel myself. These waters can be treacherous."

"Were you a fisherman then?" she asked conversationally.

He shrugged. "It's been along time since!"

"You must have had an interesting life," she remarked. After Tom had filled Naida in at great length, on his past oceanic adventures, Naida asked if she might use the bathroom to freshen up.

"Sure m'dear. There's a small cloakroom through the hall, third on the right." He got up and pointed in the direction.

Naida found the cloakroom and splashed her face with cold water. When she emerged, somewhat restored to her normal self, Tom was talking to a man outside. An old sheepdog sat panting by his side, went to bark, then thought better of it. The man glanced over at her with curiosity. His prematurely grey hair made him look like a gentleman farmer. Naida liked the look of him immediately.

She, was not from these parts, he surmised. No, her mode of dress was far too unconventional; the denim flares and embroidered peasant blouse. He labelled her a typical student backpacker from London. She fingered the brightly coloured beads around her neck nervously, not realising how out of place she appeared on a Cornish farm.

"This be Naida come to see you Ivor," explained Tom.

Naida took a deep breath to still the palpitations that threatened her composure. She said, rather too hastily, "Hello Mr. Tregartha – I – I understand you have rooms to let for the summer and was wondering if I could stay here for a few weeks. I'm an art student and want to paint the Cornish landscape. They say the light is inspiring down here." She stopped to catch her breath, concealing a torrent of emotions.

Ivor Tregartha observed her warily. She seemed highly strung. "You should have phoned first," he replied. "I used to let rooms in the holiday season, but haven't done so for some time, due to my wife's illness. Too much stress or any sudden shock could debilitate her further."

"Oh, I'm sorry – I," Naida stammered. "I didn't phone because I thought it would be easy to find somewhere to stay."

Noticing Naida's dismay, Tom interrupted. "We could put 'er up for a bit Ivor, we've plenty room – and Marianne wouldn't mind, I'm sure."

Ivor was thoughtful for a moment. There was something about the girl that was endearing. Perhaps she would prove to be just the tonic Marianne needed.

"I suppose we could," he relented. "As Tom says, we have enough rooms," Ivor took a deep breath. "Ok, it's bed and breakfast and evening meal."

"Fine, thank you," Naida said, relieved. So far her plan was going smoothly. "I'll be quiet as a mouse – you won't know I'm here."

"I hope we will," smiled Ivor.

Naida noticed his green eyes sparkle.

"We need some laughter around here," he quipped. "Come on in I'll show you to your room."

Inside, the farmhouse was long and rambling with low beamed ceilings and Tudor panelled walls. The spacious rooms exuded an air of mystery. Most people would describe it as homely. Naida, however, could sense certain things.

Ivor led her along the flagstone hall to stairs twisting up in the corner. At the top he stopped at the fourth door on the left.

"This room overlooks the fields – you can see the hills in the distance," he said, walking over to the window.

On entering, Naida had been plunged back in time. She crossed the room to the low window set in the thick whitewashed wall. Below she could see a sheltered, slate-paved walled garden. Fragrant shrubs climbed the wall.

"Yes - it's charming," she answered. The situation had become intangible.

"Right then, I shall leave you to unpack and settle in. Dinner is at seven in the dining room, if you would like to join us?" he suggested.

Naida didn't appear to hear him at first, and then turned abruptly. "Thanks, that's great." It all seemed too easy. "I think I'll rest this afternoon."

"However I must warn you my wife is an invalid. She suffers from depression and gets upset easily," he confided. "It's a nervous condition."

"Don't worry, I'll tread carefully," she promised. She had coped often enough with depression. Her Mother had suffered intermittent bouts.

Naida had a quick shower and lay on the bed for awhile. Her energies restored she took a leisurely stroll through the country lanes to find the local village. She found a quaint corner shop that seemed to sell everything from tinned food and cakes to cotton reels. She bought a pasty to take back to her room for lunch. Later in the warm evening, she changed into a floaty Indian cotton dress in shades of purple and lilac. Her recently washed hair shone, caught up at the sides with purple combs to control her curls. Slipping into her thonged sandals, she prepared to meet the Tregartha's and hoped she wasn't out of her depth. She would just take one day at a time. With one last look in the mirror, she stepped out.

A small rotund, red-faced woman was busying herself by the old range in the snug kitchen diner. She was lifting a pie dish from the cloam oven.

Ivor Tregartha was seated at the farmhouse table opposite Tom. A girl with glossy blonde hair, cut in a sharp bob, was sitting next to him. She looked about sixteen.

They stopped their chatter and glanced in Naida's direction as she entered. This made her feel like she was intruding.

Ivor spoke first. "Come in Naida and sit down. My Father Tom you've already met – and Lowenna," he gestured towards the girl, "my daughter. I'm afraid my wife is feeling unwell this evening. And this is Mrs. Dunn – our treasure," he teased, winking at the rotund woman.

"Go on with yer," Mrs. Dunn replied sourly, then nodded jovially towards Naida.

Naida's mind spun. She found herself looking down at the quarry tiled floor, then up again at the Welsh dresser. She managed to compose herself and said she was pleased to meet them all.

"You come and sit by me m' dear and make yourself at 'ome," said Tom cheerily. "We don't stand on ceremony 'ere. We're an easy going lot."

"Speak for yourself Grandpa," retorted Lowenna haughtily.

"Curb that tongue my girl," Tom reproached his Grand-daughter, like one used to her sarcasm.

Lowenna glared with suspicion at Naida, and Naida had the vague feeling that this girl was going to be trouble.

"I hope you like my Stargazy pie," said Mrs. Dunn, breaking the tension.

Naida scrutinized the fish-heads protruding from the pie crust. "I've never eaten it before," she admitted warily.

Tom laughed at her bemused expression. "You don't eat the pilchard's heads m'dear."

Naida looked relieved." I'm sure it's delicious. I love fish."

"It's a traditional Cornish dish," Mrs. Dunn informed proudly. "And the vegetables are fresh – home grown. I 'ope you're not one of those girls who don't like veggies."

"No – I eat a lot of them. Our fridge is full of salad," Naida went on flippantly; she was warming to Mrs. Dunn. "Hopefully it helps keep me trim."

"I - don't need to diet," drawled Lowenna, eyeing Naida up and down. "I suppose some find it hard to keep their figure," she threw the words out absently.

"That's enough Lowenna, where are your manners?" said her Father. "I'm sure Naida doesn't need to lose weight and you my girl, could do with helping out here a bit more – that would keep you fit!"

Lowenna shrugged and pursed her lips.

"C'mon now, no more nonsense. Let's enjoy our meal. Mrs. Dunn has done us proud," said Tom, passing the vegetable dish towards Naida.

"Do you live with your family?" asked Ivor with interest.

Naida hesitated briefly. "I live in London with my Stepfather and brother. I left college in the autumn to care for my Mother, who died recently."

"I am sorry," replied Ivor with genuine sympathy.

Naida bit her lip, and then continued with forced optimism. "I may go back to college, I don't know yet."

Tom shook his head and sighed. "You youngsters have so many more opportunities these days. It wasn't so in my youth. I bet you've travelled abroad also," he observed her closely. She looked like she had just returned from somewhere exotic – India perhaps?

"Well, I've spent most of my holidays in Cyprus," answered Naida with slight caution. He was asking too many questions.

Ivor Tregartha looked up from his plate abruptly and studied her with renewed interest.

Naida went on quickly, "Do you go abroad much?"

"I've crossed the channel in my time! But never been to London!" said Tom.

"I have travelled in the past," added Ivor, "but we've always been so busy running the farm. Now it's a lot easier – we could." Ivor looked encouraged as the thought occurred to him. "But there again, my wife may not be up to travelling."

Lowenna's sullen expression suddenly lit up. "Howard and I could come with you Pops!"

"I don't suppose Howard would have the time to go gallivanting off abroad with us, he's far too busy with his fishing trips these days," replied Ivor, then explained to Naida, "Howard's a family friend who lives in the village. He taught Lowenna to scuba dive last summer."

"That's something I would love to do again someday," said Naida. She smiled at the happy memory of her childhood holidays spent in Cyprus with her Mother's family.

At that moment the dog decided to put his paws on Naida's lap.

"Down Fenn," ordered Ivor.

"It's along time since we 'ad such charming company, isn't it boy?" beamed Tom, pushing the dog away.

"You're an old rogue Grandpa," taunted Lowenna, then added dismissively, "He says that to all our visitors. He doesn't mean it of course."

"I think it's a very nice thing for your Grandpa to say," Naida replied quietly and not waiting for a reply continued, "The pie was tasty Mrs. Dunn. I enjoyed it."

"I'm glad m' dear. I'll give you a good sample of genuine west country meals while you're here," she said. "Now if you're all finished – go and relax in the sitting room and I'll bring your coffee in."

"Lowenna, help Mrs. Dunn carry the coffee in," said Ivor.

"Do I have to? I've got so much to do, sorting out my outfit for the disco tomorrow – and I'm sure

Naida is good at that sort of thing!" she got up hurriedly and flounced out of the room before he could protest.

Ivor looked at Tom and sighed. It would be pointless to call her back and risk a tantrum in front of their guest. He would lecture her later. She was supposed to be studying for her exams.

"It's alright, I'll help with the coffee," offered Naida, overlooking Lowenna's derision.

"No need," replied Mrs. Dunn bluntly, "I can manage."

Ivor smiled. "We like our guests to feel at home. Feel free to come and go as you please and have access to the living room in the evenings."

Rising to her feet, Naida accompanied the two men into the sitting room. After they had conversed for some time, lingering over their coffee, Ivor and Tom left to secure the outbuildings for the night. Naida sat for awhile longer, gathering her thoughts. The room grew dark, the walls engulfed her. In a strange way it was comforting.

Mrs. Dunn had long since left for her cottage in the village. The house was silent. A black and white photograph of a young woman on the mantle piece caught Naida's eye. She stood up to place her cup on the side. The woman's smile, she noticed did not quite reach her eyes that seemed to follow Naida around the room. Like Alice who wanders in her underworld, thought Naida. Who was she, this woman taking refuge behind the glass? Her hair was cut short, which suited her elfin face. Naida was intrigued. However, uneasiness crept over her. Mischievous demons seemed to cringe, brooding, in

11

the dark alcoves. Echoes of sadness bounced off the cool stone tiles. And as Naida contemplated the woman's expression, she thought she heard the haunting strains of a flute across the hall.

Quickly she switched on the table lamp. The light lit the darkness through the open leaded window. Outside, in the sounds of the night, some wild animal foraged for food. The wind stirred and a rustling was heard in the trees. Naida, forgetting her problems for the moment, was unaware of being silently watched from the shadows.

Chapter 2

Naida lay awake in bed and assessed her situation. She recalled the events that had led up to her arrival at old Moorstone farm. The chilling words of her stepfather came back to haunt her, "Be ready to leave for Cyprus in the morning," he had said. She had no say in the matter that was made perfectly clear. She knew then there was no choice but to go quickly. She had, after all, managed to reach the age of twenty three still single and had no intention of being married off to a suitable Greek man like a chattel to be bought! Trying hard to put the thoughts of her stepfather Andreas out of her mind, she turned out the bedside lamp, and then fell into a sound sleep.

With the exception of Lowennas hostility, Naida soon adapted to the Tregartha family's routine. She had tucked away her past in a safe compartment of her mind. Mrs. Tregartha had not yet surfaced from her room. Mrs. Dunn was regularly seen taking a tray up to the closed door leading to the top of the house. It was very sad that on a beautiful early summer's day, Ivor's wife should feel the need to lock herself away. It was cruel as dead autumn leaves no more to tease the sun, mused Naida.

Naida spent much of her time walking the wild countryside and sketching. Tom accompanied her occasionally. She enjoyed his company. He would talk forever on the subject of his Cornwall, but when she probed a little about the family and Mrs. Tregartha's condition, he was evasive.

Today Tom had taken Naida to Prussia Cove. The descent from the car park to the small area of beach was a little awkward. Naida held on to Tom to make sure neither of them slipped.

"We'll 'ave to move to the rocks when the tide comes in," Tom informed her as they found a spot to sit. "I like to watch 'em fishing 'ere and the views good."

It was peaceful in the brilliant sunshine. However, Naida visualised the wind whipping the waves against the rocks later in the day. "It's certainly rugged. I shouldn't think it's suitable for bathing," she remarked.

"No, you 'ave to take care swimming near the rocks," replied Tom. "This spot was once the haunt of a notorious smuggler you know – John Carter, who was called the King of Prussia by his associates. Oh yes, there's many a tale o' smuggling in these parts."

"Really! Tell me more Tom, I can almost feel it." Naida was intrigued as she imagined how it was a century ago, with the tide up on a dark night.

"Tomorrow I'll take you to Loe Bar and Porthleven," suggested Tom, enjoying her enthusiasm. "Now, there's a place seen many a shipwreck in the past."

This appealed to the romantic adventurer in Naida. "Are they still down at the bottom of the ocean?"

"Could be," replied Tom. "Winter storms caused sailing ships of last century to flounder. And in the early nineteen hundreds many gold coins were discovered by locals on the beach."

Naida looked surprised. "If any are left they're probably buried deep in the sand by now." She took out her pad and began to sketch.

Tom nodded, "It was soon nicknamed the goldmine. Semi-precious stones separate an inland pool from the sea."

"I would love to go there – it sounds fascinating. You never know we might find a coin or two!" she joked and presumed it would be like finding a needle in a haystack.

"If you're interested in smugglers tales, you should talk to Howard Elliot, 'es descended from the buccaneer Henry Elliot, whose ship it is said, was wrecked near Church Cove in the eighteenth century – carrying gold bars."

"Howard?" she turned to face Tom. "You mean the family friend?"

"Yes, he often comes to the farm. I expect you'll get to meet 'im."

Until late afternoon Naida sat sketching the fishermen, content to listen to Tom's soft dialect. Her concentration wandered from time to time to the intriguing Howard Elliot. She built up a fanciful picture of him in her vivid imagination.

By the time they had arrived back at the farm, Naida had mused over all the possibilities as to Howard Elliot's character. First she imagined him short and stocky, with rakish pirate's features, brash – loud – unruly. By the time she was sitting on the wooden bench below her window in the walled garden, waiting for dinner, he had grown taller in her estimation. Soft brown hair and blue eyes mocked her.

Something made her look up to the small window in the attic. Close to the glass a woman was watching her. She recognised her face as the girl she had seen in the photo frame in the living room. But now she looked older, her light brown hair quite silver around the temples. So this was Mrs. Marianne Tregartha.

Naida smiled and waved. The woman looked straight through her, hollow eyed and sad. A coldness crept over Naida, despite the warmth of the evening. Then the woman's eyes focused on her. She gave a faint smile and raised her hand slowly, as if she intended to wave back. Behind her, a figure appeared and quickly closed the curtains.

The following morning Tom was suffering from exhaustion. Naida thought it was probably due to too much sun yesterday.

"We'll 'ave to postpone our trip to Porthleven until later," he told her with regret.

She decided to take the trip by herself and perhaps take a swim. The sun was hot as she headed for the bus stop.

Alighting at Porthleven, Naida walked to a small beach below the pier. She placed her towel on the sand and slipped out of her shorts and tee shirt to reveal a white bandeau bikini. This caused many admiring glances. She walked to the waters edge, sinking her toes into the wet sand and breathed in the salty air. Gradually she eased her way in until the water reached her waist. It was shockingly cool. Holding her breath, she dived in. This was near to heaven, she thought, gliding effortlessly.

Exhilarated, she emerged and went back up the beach to laze on her towel. She dozed for awhile before sitting up to eat her lunch. Gazing southwards, areas of rock and sand reached all the way to Loe Pool. The only way to get there on foot was the cliff path that ran alongside the bar.

Late afternoon she decided to walk the distance. She dressed again and set off, glad of her trainers. It was rough going. Eventually she gained access to the rocks below. Plenty of grassy areas provided her with a place to sit. Shafts of sunlight coloured the sea lapis lazuli. Prisms split rays mesmerised her as they danced on the waves. Naida imagined she heard the sea calling her in.

So absorbed in frivolous thoughts was she, that she failed to see the notice – DANGER STRONG CURRENTS. She undressed once more and lowered herself from the bank. She swam out, diving and ducking, fish-like, deep underwater, coming up for air, floating on her back, then down she went again. Always she felt at home in the sea, never having cause to fear. In Cyprus they had nicknamed her "little fish." Time lost all meaning. Surfacing finally, she glanced back and couldn't make out where exactly she had drifted to. However, she was not too alarmed and began swimming towards the rocks.

Suddenly the pressure of the water was fighting against her. The beach shelved steeply. She found herself pulled in the opposite direction and to her horror had no control. Terror seized her as she realised her predicament. She shrieked for help, but the shoreline was deserted at this spot and with blind panic, felt herself pulled beneath the waves.

Down, down she descended, her mind strangely detached. The ocean roared in her head. She managed to struggle to the surface and frantically aimed for a jutting rock. If only she could reach it she would be safe. Luckily the current pushed her in the right direction.

Making a desperate attempt, she hauled herself up and found, to her relief, enough room to sit. Having gained some degree of safety, she now wondered how long she could stay there before the incoming tide.

Naida huddled on her refuge for what seemed to her like hours. She was becoming increasingly uneasy as the water splashed ever higher against the rock. It was frustrating to hear the whir of boats out of her vision. The faint scudding across the water was growing louder. Out of the blue distance the approaching shape became clearer. She called out. "Over here!"

As the boat drew closer, the man on board shouted. "What do you think you are – a mermaid?"

The sarcasm of his tongue cut jagged through her ultra sensitised state. He came alongside, reaching out muscular arms. "Catch hold of my hands," he demanded.

There was nothing else she could do but obey.

He pulled her roughly into the boat and bellowed at her above the roar of the waves. "You little fool. If I hadn't come by you would have drowned."

Indignant that this man should speak to her so sharply, she flushed scarlet. To make matters worse, she could not help but notice how ruggedly attractive he was.

Trying to gather some dignity the best she could under the circumstances, she retorted, "I was perfectly alright thank you. I'm sure I could have swum to the shore!"

"Don't be ridiculous!" he stormed, eyes blazing. "Have you any idea how dangerous these currents are? You tourists come down here and put everyone's lives at risk," he reprimanded sternly, making her tremble. "Men have been swept away, never to be seen again!"

Angry at her own stupidity, Naida made no attempt to argue. Tears threatened as she sat in silence until they reached the shore. Jumping awkwardly out of the boat, she mumbled a thank you and went to head on up the beach.

"Where do you think you're going in that state?" he barked after her.

"There's nothing wrong with me. I'll be fine now," she attempted to hide her vulnerability, only too aware of her near nakedness in the skimpy bikini.

His penetrating steel blue eyes bore right into her. "Stop and wait there," he ordered, "I'll just moor the boat and then I'll see you home."

Naida ignored him and carried on up the beach. She began to shiver, her hair clinging flatly to her head. At this moment she wished she had the power to magic herself invisible.

He secured the boat and then with long strides caught up with her. "Don't be stubborn, you'll catch pneumonia. Look at least let me fetch your clothes.

Here, take my sweater." His voice was forceful and she no longer had the strength to oppose him.

A sudden dizziness sent her stumbling against him.

"Here," he offered her his sweater and wrapped it around her shoulders, then said a little more gently, "Show me where your clothes are and then we had better get back to where you are staying."

"I left them on the grass at Loe Pool," she answered lamely and didn't resist as he steadied her along the beach. The touch of his hand on her arm felt oddly reassuring, until they reached the area.

"He stopped suddenly and turned on her accusingly. "Can't you read?" He pointed towards the DANGER notice with contempt.

Naida gasped, realising her foolish mistake. Severely humiliated she gritted her teeth.

His strong jaw set in disbelief. He picked up her clothes, almost throwing them at her and demanded, "Where are you staying?"

"At Perranuthnoe," she whispered, very near to collapsing.

He led her to his car parked nearby in Loe Bar and in stony silence drove her back to Old Moorstone Farm.

On arrival Naida thanked him with icy politeness. Letting herself in, she went straight to her room. Cocooning herself under the bed covers never felt more inviting. As soon as her head hit the pillow she was out like a light. Fitfully she dreamed of her Mother calling her from a long tunnel…. warning her.

Next morning the activity centred, as usual, around the farmhouse kitchen table. Mrs Dunn was pouring the tea. Lowenna was in the hall talking on the telephone. Naida's thoughts were still full of last nights dream. She was trying hard to remember the details without much success, when Mrs Dunn's voice snapped her back to the present moment.

"Lowenna," she called, Come and drink this tea while it's hot."

Lowenna replaced the telephone receiver. "Hey – great news," she enthused. A furtive smile played on her lips. "That was Howard."

I 'eard he was back," said Mrs Dunn. "Some of the locals are holding a barbecue for 'im tonight."

"Yes I know," replied Lowenna, "he just phoned to say everyone's invited – well almost everyone," she added with an edge of disdain.

"In that case you must come too Naida," said Tom, looking up from his morning newspaper.

Lowennas features set sharply. "I don't think it will be her cup of tea."

"No, I have a letter to write anyway," stressed Naida, not particularly in the mood to face a lot of strangers after her ordeal at Loe Bar.

"Nonsense girl," said Tom, briskly folding his newspaper. "You 'aven't met any young people since you've been 'ere. It will do you good."

"If she says she can't go – she can't go Grandpa," snapped Lowenna.

Tom winked at Naida. "I won't 'ear any excuses."

Naida was touched by his concern. She knew it would please him if she went. Lowenna had no right to intimidate her. "I guess I can write my letter another time."

"You do look tired Naida," remarked Ivor. He hadn't heard her come in last night. It must have been late.

"I feel okay. The sea air tires you and I got to bed late." Naida picked up her spoon and toyed with her cereal.

Lowenna studied her curiously and then asked her in a forthright manner. "Where did you go?"

"I spent the day on the beach and later had a look around Porthleven. Then I decided to have a meal in town." Naida bent the truth a little. She had no intention of being open to ridicule from Lowenna or of worrying the others. The whole incident was best forgotten, put behind her like a bad dream and anyway, she was unlikely to come across that detestable man again, she thought wryly.

Thankfully no more questions were asked. The conversation turned to the tasks to be done. It was market day, a busy day for the men. Ivor and Tom finished their breakfast and went out to the smallholding. Mrs Dunn cleared away the dishes. Lowenna stretched her arms above her head and yawned.

Eyeing Naida haughtily, she said, "I must go into town today and see if I can buy something special to wear for the barbecue."

"For a barbecue?" replied Naida doubtfully, "I would have thought it would be casual clothes."

"Oh no," drawled Lowenna, "This is to be a gala occasion – a dressy affair. If I was you I'd search through that haversack of yours and dig out something upmarket." She tilted her head pertly to one side and played with her hair. "That's if you own such a thing."

Naida refused to rise to the bait. "I'm sure I can come up with something," she answered with quiet dignity.

"Otherwise," went on Lowenna airily, "I'm afraid you will be completely out of place – believe me." She got up to go, leaving Naida perplexed.

Mid-day, Mrs Dunn offered to make Naida lunch before she left. There would be no need for her to prepare dinner for the evening. Therefore she was off to get ready for the barbecue.

Naida decided it was time to search through her haversack, as Lowenna had so scornfully suggested. As she passed by the living room, she was surprised to see a woman hovering by the bookshelf. At the sound of Naida's footsteps the woman spun round abruptly. Her expression held the look of a thief caught in the act. Recognising Marianne Tregartha, Naida took a step into the room to greet her.

Marianne backed away, the look in her eyes spoke pure terror.

"Hello," said Naida gently, "I'm Naida – I'm staying here as a guest. You must be Marianne."

Marianne did not answer. She held on so tightly to the bookcase the whiteness of her knuckles protruded.

This odd behaviour unnerved Naida; she wasn't sure how to react. However, instinct took over and she took a step backwards.

"I saw you at your window," Naida tried again.

Marianne let go of the bookcase and peered curiously at Naida. "You waved to me," she whispered, then quickly backed away again. "How do I know you are who you say?"

"I'm sorry if I startled you. I'll go if you like," Naida turned to the door.

"No!" The single word echoed weakly, like a cry for help.

Naida stopped, turned around and waited.

"No," repeated Marianne, "Don't go – you – you're not one of them – are you?" she said falteringly.

"Pardon?" replied Naida, "one of whom?"

"I can tell you're good," Marianne stated eyes wide.

"You can?" asked Naida. The woman was mentally unbalanced. She was far more disturbed than Naida had been led to believe. It was perhaps best to humour her.

"It was nice of you to wave to me. A lot of people aren't nice." Marianne spoke wistfully, and then became agitated. "But you'd better not let them see you here with me."

"Who? Who mustn't see me?" wondered Naida.

Marianne pressed her lips together and shook her head. She had retreated back into her shell. Footsteps were heard approaching. Naida glanced out of the window. Lowenna passed by on her way back from the town. As she turned the key in the front door, Marianne, quick as lightning, brushed past Naida and scurried upstairs to her room.

Chapter 3

Naida combed her hair and left it to dry naturally, after her shower, before sweeping it up. She was filled with excited anticipation at the thought of meeting the mysterious Howard Elliot. To her mind it seemed unorthodox to dress up for a barbecue, however she assumed Lowenna was more acquainted with these local social gatherings.

It was lucky she had included in her luggage her two designer dresses. She held up an off the shoulder number in fuchsia pink. Having stuffed it hurriedly into her rucksack, it needed a good shake. The dress fell back into place beautifully. The classic lines accentuated her slim figure. She slipped on her wedge mules, then applied a matching fuchsia lip gloss, took one last look in the mirror and stepped out confidently as Ivor gave an impatient honk on the car horn.

Tom beamed at Naida admiringly. "Don't she look a picture?" he said.

Lowenna, who was trying hard to adjust a straight face, let out a muffled laugh.

"What's amused you madam?" asked her Father.

"Nothing," she smirked.

As Naida got into the car she saw Lowenna was dressed in shorts and tee shirt like the others. A surge of anger arose within her as she realised the joke at her expense.

"I thought tonight was to be a dressy occasion?" she asked curtly.

"No, but you look gorgeous m' darlin'," answered Tom.

Lowenna frowned. Perhaps she had made a fatal mistake in her bid to make Naida look foolish. It seemed to be backfiring.

Awkwardly, Naida fingered her hair, swept up in a perfect French pleat. She glanced down at her outfit. She was beginning to feel like an overdressed Christmas tree. "Why did you tell me to dress up?" she remonstrated. "I can't possibly go like this!"

"It was only a joke. I don't know what you're getting so het up about," Lowenna demurred sulkily.

"How could you?" Ivor glared at his daughter, who sat petulantly with her chin resting on her palm. "I'll have a word to say about this later my girl. I'm sorry Naida, Lowenna has obviously been up to her pranks again."

Lowenna looked unperturbed.

"Anyway, there's no time to change," said Ivor, driving off before Naida could protest. "Don't worry; you'll knock 'em dead tonight."

This proved to be true, much to Lowenna's annoyance.

Naida soon found herself enjoying the easy going acceptance of the young people. Nobody made her feel out of place. The local girls complemented her on her dress and asked her questions about the exciting city life they imagined she led.

It seemed the entire village had turned out for the party. The drink flowed freely and the atmosphere became highly charged with gaiety. In light hearted banter, Naida threw her head back and laughed. At that precise moment she caught sight of Lowenna under a towering tree with her arm linked possessively through the arm of a good looking man. He was dressed in casual khaki jeans and shirt. He appeared to be the centre of attention.

With an uncanny sense of being watched, he turned. His eyes met Naida's. With a half sardonic smile curving his lips, he nodded. She stopped laughing abruptly. It was that damn man again, she realised with shock. So this is Howard Elliot. She looked away, for some reason his presence made her heart pound. How stupid, she chided herself. She couldn't stand the man and anyway Lowenna obviously had designs on him.

Somehow the evening seemed to fall flat. What on earth was the matter with her, she wondered, to let that awful man affect her so? Why had she idealised him in her mind as some romantic hero? Her vivid imagination would be her undoing. She was about to lose herself in the crowd, when Tom put his arm lightly around her shoulders and said. "Naida, I want you to meet our friend Howard. Lowenna seems to have claimed 'im for the evening. Unfair I think, don't you?"

He steered her over towards them and Naida, feeling uncomfortable, had no choice but to accompany him.

"Howard, meet our charming guest from London – Naida," said Tom, introducing them.

When Howard first set eyes on Naida this evening, he was amazed at the transformation from the bedraggled girl of last night. He was impressed. She was stunning, if unsuitably dressed.

"Hi there! If it isn't the mermaid," he mocked in that disturbingly deep voice. "Been washed up on any rocks lately?"

To have the power to magically disappear again was prevalent in her thoughts at this moment. With an effort to sound nonchalant, she answered, "No, but if I should, I'm sure I could swim to safety without any help from you." Her tone was witty, not wanting to inflame the situation.

"You've already met I see," said Tom in surprise.

"Yes – we met on the beach yesterday," hedged Naida. She prayed Howard would not elaborate.

"That's right Tom – I – gave her a lift in the boat from Porthleven to Loe Bar," cut in Howard, tongue in cheek.

"Good – I'll leave you young people to enjoy yourselves. Lowenna go and fetch your Father, I think we 'ad better be making tracks home soon. Your Mother will fret if we're too late" urged Tom. "You stay awhile longer Naida. I'm sure Howard will run you home."

Naida glanced despairingly at Tom. His intentions were good, but in all innocence he was compromising her.

"No, I'll come - ," she began.

"No problem," Howard insisted loudly. "I'll make sure she's back before the witching hour."

Lowenna clenched her teeth with concealed rage. She was only too aware of how radiant Naida looked and how her practical joke had most definitely backfired. Reluctantly she did as Tom said. Naida was left to face Howard alone.

She stood erect and looked Howard straight in the eye. "I suppose I should thank you for not letting on about my escapade," she said begrudgingly.

"Don't worry your secret is safe with me. I wouldn't want to embarrass you and expose you foolishness. Come now sweet mermaid I'll get you a drink before you disappear into the ocean," he said teasingly. "What shall it be?"

Damn him I'll never live this down," she thought. He would not succeed in flustering her though. She would not give him the satisfaction.

"I'll stick to the punch please," she answered loosely.

He raised his eyebrows. "I would have thought a more sophisticated drink would suit you."

"Why?" she asked primly, tossing her head back.

"You look like you're used to the high life!" He eyed her up and down insolently. "I'll take you out on my boat sometime. Girls here on holiday often ask to sunbathe topless on deck."

What infuriating conceit! He's insufferable! I suppose he thinks he just has to click his fingers and get any girl to jump to his command.

"No thank you, I'm not the slightest bit interested," she grimaced. "There's no way I would sunbathe topless on your boat!"

He let her remark pass and went to fetch her drink. She glanced around. There was still quite a crowd. Naida watched him ladle the punch into the glass. A group of girls had gathered around him, like bees to a honey pot, each one vying for his attention. It was clear he was popular. Men came up and patted him on the back. They were full of jovial mood and Naida heard one say. "Still one for the girls, eh Howard," and someone else added, "I bet you've got a girl notched up in every port."

Naida turned away. She didn't want him to catch her looking. So! He has quite a reputation, has he? She thought. I must keep a wide berth from this one.

He managed to untangle himself from the group and made his way over to Naida with her drink. "Sorry I was so long. They wouldn't leave me alone," he grinned.

"Is that so?" she replied disinterestedly.

He laughed at her coolness, and then winked wickedly. "You should think yourself privileged to have me all to yourself."

"Hm, Really?" She replied with cool indifference, thinly masking her emotions.

He put his drink down carefully and straightened up to his full height. Naida leaned back against the tree. If she had been looking into his eyes she might have been forewarned. However, she had lowered her head level to the expansion of his chest. Hard, taut muscle strained the buttons on his shirt, blocking her vision, causing her to catch her breath. Against her own skin the large oak dug into her back.

Suddenly, his arms were either side of her, trapping her. "Come now, I don't believe you're as icy cold as you appear. I bet I could melt you!"

The close proximity of his masculine scent unnerved Naida. He was obviously enjoying her reactions. He was mocking her. For a moment she was thwarted, looking up into his playful steel blue eyes. Then the survival instinct took over. She raised her arms to push him away. The impact had no effect.

"Let me go!" She snapped.

"He raised an eyebrow. "Is that what you really want?" He breathed, his eyes still held hers, testing her reaction.

She was speechless. He hadn't blinked once. Who the hell did he think he was to actually believe she was lying? She wondered what he intended to do next. However, this was cut short by the approach of two men. Howard turned to see who was coming, allowing Naida a reprieve.

As the men came close, one clasped Howard's hand. "You are one in a million," he enthused.

"The same goes for me," said the other.

"It was nothing," Howard replied modestly. "I just happened to be in a position to help, that's all. I don't like to see my friends at the mercy of some unscrupulous property developers. I'll fight anyone who threatens our village."

Whatever it was he had done, Howard was evidently held in high esteem around here. So the man has feelings, thought Naida. What was he, some sort of Jekyll and Hyde? Well that doesn't prove a thing. I will no longer continue with this charade.

She took the opportunity to escape and went to see if there was any food left. For about an hour she mingled with the guests and accepted another glass of punch. She began to feel light headed. It was getting late. The last bus had already gone. She had no option but to swallow her pride, go and find Howard and take him up on his offer.

The drink had loosened her inhibitions. She had not realised just how strong the local punch was. Swaying up behind Howard, she had the sudden urge to ridicule him.

"What is this do in aid of tonight – the Howard Elliot appreciation society?" She hiccupped. "Yes - I bet you have enticed many an unsuspecting female onto your boat. Am I right Howard Elliot? I suppose you think you are the Don Juan of Peranuthnoe. Well, here's one female who isn't impressed," she taunted mercilessly. "It's been a most interesting evening – I would like to leave now."

As she spun around precariously, he swiftly caught her by surprise. He supported her firmly encircling her waist. "You deserve to be chastised for your reckless behaviour," he threatened. "But on the other hand, you're lucky the evening has mellowed me."

They stood alone, hidden from the remaining few by the large oak. Looking menacingly into her startled green eyes, he lowered his face and then kissed her, long and hard. Temporarily the world spun. She seemed to be sinking into her own heavenly oblivion. Finally, the unexpected harshness of the kiss sent her into a state of shock and left her reeling.

"Is that what you want, my mermaid." He whispered huskily, studying her. Then he loosened his grip. "I think I had better get you home."

She crumpled against the tree, too dazed to answer or protest when he lifted her up into his strong arms and carried her gently to his car. Naida's head was spinning from the effects of the alcohol. He drove her back down the narrow winding lanes in silence. The steady hum of the engine filled the black night.

Howard pulled up at the farm, got out and accompanied Naida to the front door. She rummaged through her bag for her key. Opening the door she switched on the hall light then flopped ungainly onto a chair.

"It looks like I'll have to carry you to your room," he said, gathering her into his arms once again. "Where is it?"

"Upstairs, fourth on the left," she managed.

Next morning Naida awoke with a throbbing head. The dazzling sun assaulted her eyes through the crack in the curtains. She groaned and shielded them with her hand. Then flashes of last night came rushing back. She remembered being carried to her room. But then what? She must have passed out.

Looking down, she realised she was naked. Her clothes were draped across the chair. Surely he hadn't undressed her? The thought alarmed her initially. Surprisingly a surge of something akin to excitement shot through her. She stretched out in the bed and began massaging her temples to soothe her aching head.

She then placed her hands on her solar plexus to calm her fluttering nerves and thought of Howard. The taut hardness of his chest made her quiver. And oh my God, that kiss! A secret smile curved her lips. It was time for breakfast. She slipped out of bed and put on her shorts and tee shirt. She must stop thinking of Howard like this; he was obviously a player, not the sort of man to get involved with without being hurt.

"Mornin' Naida – beautiful day. How are you feeling? Enjoy yourself last night, did you?" asked Tom keenly, as she sat down opposite him at the kitchen table.

Naida poured some coffee into her cup. "I'm feeling a bit fragile this morning. It must have been that punch I was drinking."

"Oh m' dear, I should have warned you about that – its lethal stuff if you overdo it." Tom rolled his eyes. "God knows what they put in it. Good job you were with Howard eh? I left you in good 'ands," he nodded, then continued," Any plans for today?"

"Not really. I was wondering if Ivor needed any help in the smallholding. Otherwise I'll have to look around for a seasonal job fruit picking or something. The money I brought with me is running low."

"Ivor always needs help in the orchard – and with deliveries – you just ask 'im. He's up and working already. Go and see him after breakfast," suggested Tom, and then asked," and what do you think of our Howard then?"

Naida felt the colour creep to her cheeks. "I – um – well I haven't met a fisherman like him before," she answered evasively.

"The poor boy 'as 'ad a hard time of it since his parents died when he was only fifteen. Ivor and Marianne took him in – Marianne was different then. She looked after 'im like her own."

"How awful," said Naida, stunned.

"He was of course devastated and ever since then 'es been like family to us and Lowenna thinks of 'im as her brother. When 'e came of age 'e decided to go back to 'is old cottage, Tamarose, in the village. He lives there now when 'es not away on fishing trips."

"What happened to his parents?" asked Naida. She was starting to feel some empathy for him and perhaps regret her behaviour.

"It was a tragedy. His own mother, father and uncle, good friends of ours, were swept away at sea." Tom ran his fingers through his course white hair and sighed. "They were attempting to rescue a man. He wasn't a local and misjudged the currents."

"Dreadful!" Naida shook her head in disbelief. "How sad – what a terrible thing to happen." No wonder he was so incensed when he discovered her marooned on that rock. Perhaps that's the reason for his apparent cynicism, she thought.

"Its thirteen years ago now since it 'appened and as they say, time heals, but it's something 'e will carry inside 'im forever." Tom straightened up. After a moment's reflection he added, "Any way, we mustn't dwell on the past. It won't do none of us any good and certainly not Howard."

35

Early Monday morning Naida made her way to the smallholding to get acquainted with the surroundings. Ivor, who had been into town, drove up in the land rover. He parked in a good position for loading and then sat watching Naida thoughtfully. It had been agreed between them that she could help him deliver the fruit and vegetable produce for the rest of the season. He got out and walked towards her.

"Morning Naida. Bright and early I see," he called.

"Hello Ivor, yes, it's such a lovely day, I couldn't wait to start," she answered smiling.

"Good, I'll show you what has to be done today, and then take you into the village to deliver the produce. Afterwards you should be able to go on your own. It won't be too difficult once you become familiar with the area."

She nodded. "Fine – I passed my driving test last year and would love to try out the land rover."

"I'm sure you'll be ok," replied Ivor. He admired her independent spirit. "First I'll show you the different types of vegetables we grow."

Naida followed as he explained each one as they went. They came to an orchard. Beyond, cornfields stretched for miles. The peaceful tranquillity was broken only by the occasional mooing of a cow and the swish of the sea in the distance. Naida acknowledged an inner calmness of spirit she had never acquired in the city.

Later, Ivor allowed her to drive the land rover, loaded with produce, into the village. She drove expertly with him beside her giving encouragement.

"Not bad!" he praised her, confidant with her capability. "We are quite a team, aren't we?"

Her conscience made her laugh nervously. "I think I'm going to enjoy this job. It should be fun."

Ivor looked amused. "I hope so, but you may find its hard work too."

The next call was to Mrs Dunn's cottage. She was so pleased to have a visitor that she insisted Naida stay for a cup of tea. Ivor announced his next delivery was to Howard and he would return later. Naida was only too grateful to remain there under the circumstances. She followed Mrs Dunn into the kitchen.

"I'll make the tea m'dear," she said, putting the kettle on. "Then we can sit in the garden if you like and 'ave a chat."

"Okay - I'd like that," answered Naida. She had avoided facing Howard today, but knew that she couldn't elude him forever.

Mrs Dunn, like Tom, relished in a good gossip. Soon Naida was well informed with just about everyone's life history in the village, in between Mrs Dunn's ailments and recent aches and pains.

"Don't you go getting old m'dear it's not much fun'" she advised frankly. She then asked, "You enjoying your stay at Old Moorstone then?"

"Yes I am. Everyone has been so kind," answered Naida. "But there is something - it's just – I find it strange that Mrs Tregartha keeps to her room. I saw her downstairs only once and she was acting really odd."

Mrs Dunn poured the tea. "Well – I'll tell you. They've been good to me, the Tregartha's. I wouldn't say a word against them. Mrs Tregartha, well, she's suffered a lot. I'm not one to gossip mind."

Naida suppressed a smile and then looked serious. "What a shame – poor woman. I guess she's had a tough life."

"Oh yes – she's suffered that one!" repeated Mrs Dunn.

Naida sensed Mrs Dunn was finding it hard to withhold a story.

Finally it was too much for her. "She nearly died giving birth to Lowenna. That's when Lowenna's Father ran off with another woman – never was no good. "

"Ran off with another woman?" This surprised Naida. She wondered what startling revelation she was about to hear next.

"You see I shouldn't tell you this but Mr Tregartha isn't Lowenna's Father," went on Mrs Dunn with a knowing look.

Naida reclined back in her chair. "I see."

"Then they had a son, Derwin – a little angel – a musical child – only eight when he caught a rare bone disease and passed away. Mrs Tregartha found that she couldn't 'ave any more children. Such a tragedy for a homely woman like 'er – and Lowenna – so headstrong – and spoilt I'd say- still you can't blame 'em, it's understandable. Then awhile back Mrs Tregartha began suffering from depression – agoraphobia I think they call it."

"So that's it," replied Naida. That explained a lot.

"It's 'er cross to bear. I've 'elped all I can – been glad o' the work too. It's been 'ard work for them, running that farm. Still, it's eased up now, since they finished with the farming and Mr Tregartha only runs the smallholding." Mrs Dunn stopped to catch her breath.

"How long has Mrs Tregartha been agoraphobic?" asked Naida.

"Oh – a good year or so I'd say."

"You mean to tell me no one has tried to coax her out of it? It is curable you know," stressed Naida.

"The local doctor did all he could. Then Lowenna brought in some people she said would help," Mrs Dunn looked doubtful. "But after that she seemed to get worse."

Naida looked concerned. "What people?"

"Healers – herbalists I think," replied Mrs Dunn, unsure. "Of course when that didn't work the rumour was she'd gone mad. Some folk round here can be mighty superstitious."

"Um," Naida murmured thoughtfully. She came from a long line of healers and herbalists herself and had seen miracles happen. However, if the intention was to harm….

So engrossed were they in their conversation, they didn't notice Lowenna riding her bicycle past the fence. Lowenna was about to ride on, when she saw a man behind a bush looking towards the cottage. Laying down her bicycle, she crept forward for a better view. Mrs Dunn and Naida were still talking in the garden. Lowenna waited until the man eventually retreated back down the lane. Intrigued, she picked up her bicycle and continued home.

Chapter 4

Halfway along the lane, on their way back, Ivor said to Naida. "We have been invited to Howard's for dinner this evening, you too Naida."

This took her by surprise. The last thing she wanted was to see Howard Elliot tonight. In the harsh light of day she was confused by the feelings he had invoked in her.

"Oh – I was hoping to stay in this evening and finish a drawing I've been working on," she said guardedly.

"You can do that any time. Please come," coaxed Ivor, "You know, I haven't spoken to you much about my wife. As you've probably gathered, she's very reclusive – Howard and I have devised a plan to bring her out of her shell." He turned to Naida. "I understand that you spoke to her in the living room. She has spoken of nothing else since. She took to you incredibly."

Naida shot him a quick glance. "I really don't see what I can do."

"The thing is – we are going to try and get her to come this evening and I don't think we will succeed without you. If you're there it will make all the difference."

"Why?" Naida asked stalling.

"I'm sure she wants to talk to you. I have the feeling this could be a breakthrough."

Naida bit her lip in apprehension. "I still don't understand."

"Trust me. Stranger things have been known to cure a person?" He awaited her answer expectantly.

Naida sighed. He was counting on her. She felt obliged to say, "Well – in that case I can hardly refuse."

Ivor smiled, "It's settled then."

Back at the farmhouse, Lowenna was sitting in the kitchen. Ivor informed her of their plans. Her brow creased into a frown. She expelled her breath slowly, her hand smoothing down her precision cut bob.

"I don't think we should take Mother," she said. "Also Howard invites us because we are like family. He wouldn't want outsiders. It wouldn't be the same."

"We've discussed it and Naida has been invited – so don't you go spoiling the evening," Ivor admonished. "Your Mother needs your help too."

Lowenna jumped to her feet and glared at her Father. "You'll be sorry, Mother's not up to it."

"That's enough. She's coming and that's the end of it," stated Ivor. "We'll have to make sure she's alright – okay?"

A sulky expression set Lowennas features. She rounded on Naida and said slyly, "Anyway, who was that man watching you in Mrs Dunn's garden today?"

"What are you talking about?" asked Naida, suspecting another of Lowennas practical jokes.

"I don't know – just a man," snapped Lowenna impatiently, "black hair – swarthy skin – foreign looking."

42

Naida went cold and Ivor said, "I shouldn't be at all surprised Lowenna. After all, Naida is a very pretty girl!

"Hmm!" snorted Lowenna as she turned to leave, slamming the door with a thud.

It couldn't possibly be true. The girl was a compulsive liar and had a vivid imagination, Naida reasoned.

"I'm going to have a talk with Marianne now to give her plenty of time to prepare," Ivor cut through her thoughts.

Naida jumped, "Yes – and by the way, what should I wear? I don't want to make any more mistakes."

"Howard likes to make an occasion of it on his return from a trip. You can bet your life Lowenna will be dressed up to the nines," he replied.

"Okay, I'll go and get ready. "Naida pushed back her hair and went to take a shower.

Perched on the velvet covered stall, wrapped in a fluffy white towel, Naida combed through her freshly washed hair. Carefully she applied a little mousse and weaved the sides. Twisting it into a long braid, she coiled it at the nape of her neck. The style flattered her clear carved bones. A light touch of makeup enhanced her features.

She surveyed her reflection critically in the mirror, and sighed. This evening with Howard was going to be tiresome. Still, at least she had made an effort, which boosted her self esteem. The long aqua silk strapless dress she chose to wear brushed deliciously against her skin. She grabbed her bag, took a revitalizing deep breath and went out to meet the others.

They were all waiting in the living room. Ivor had his arm protectively around his wife's shoulders. She stood timidly beside him, her haunting eyes darting back and forth. To everyone's surprise her face lit up at the sight of Naida. She took a step forward.

"Oh you look divine," she exclaimed in a thin voice.

Naida had the sudden urge to give her a hug. She didn't want to cause her alarm, so instead she just said, "Thank you Mrs Tregartha." Her glance swept over the others present. "We all seem to look our best this evening."

Lowenna glared back, unimpressed. On no account was she going to be friendly towards Naida. "Howard always likes this dress on me," she snarled.

"It suits you," offered Naida.

Lowenna looked irritated. "I guess I have the figure for it." She pouted precociously with her bright scarlet lips; her youthful body slim as a reed in the clingy red mini dress, exposing a great expanse of slender legs.

Tamarose was situated at the end of a long drive, which continued past the cottage and sloped down to the sand. As they opened the gate, the sea breeze flowed gently through the tall cottage garden flowers. Naida breathed in their perfume and re-captured the magic of many summers. Other scents of the earth, soft delicate herbs, wafted, moved by the wind.

Inside, the aroma of fresh baked bread took over their sense of smell, sharpening their appetites. Howard welcomed them and ushered them to the table. Naida considered how compelling he looked, dressed in beige trousers and cream open necked shirt; his tawny hair matching his tanned skin.

He stood up to fetch more wine from the fridge and almost had to stoop in the doorway. He must be at least six foot, she thought. She couldn't deny the unsettling effect of his animal magnetism – a certain unpolished appeal. She had to admit the meal was delicious. He was too damn perfect, she conceded.

"Howard, can I have more wine please?" Lowenna leaned towards him, looking up from beneath her fluttering eyelashes in contrived innocence.

"Don't drink it so fast," said Ivor, "you're supposed to sip it slowly."

Lowenna grimaced petulantly. "But I've only had one glass."

Howard drew the cork from the bottle. "Okay – how about you Marianne – do you want your glass topped up?"

"Please," Marianne said quietly, glancing nervously at Lowenna.

"I think you've had enough Mother," snapped Lowenna, her expression icy.

Without a word, Howard tilted the bottle, filling Marianne's glass. He then proceeded to top up the others. Lowennas face set rigid. She allowed no emotion to show.

As Howard drained the last drop, she smiled at him seductively. "Will you teach me how to prepare your seafood sauce?" she asked.

"Sure," he answered lightly.

While Ivor and Tom were engrossed talking to Marianne, Lowenna leant forward and said in a low voice. "I can do wonders with mayonnaise."

Howard seemed not to have heard and turned his attention to Naida. "What about you Naida, do you like to cook, or is it all takeaways and pre-packed microwave meals in London?"

"Yes I do cook actually," Naida answered indignantly. "My Mother taught me to cook some exotic dishes."

"Oh well," cut in Lowenna, "Howard doesn't like all that foreign food. You can't beat good country cooking can you Howard?"

"I'm not so sure about that Lowenna," replied Howard, his eyes fixed squarely on Naida, making her feel uncomfortable.

"Umm, I suppose being a fisherman, you must know all about cooking fish, so you have the advantage over me," Naida said, flustered.

"You reckon us fishermen are experts, do you?" His eyes bore right through her. He was mocking her. For a moment she was lost for words, giving Lowenna the upper hand.

"Well, I know you are an expert Howard, but what would a city girl like her have in common with us?" Lowennas arm was now draped over his shoulder. They both focused their attention on Naida.

"Let's test her," hissed Lowenna.

"Okay city girl. How do you cook a freshly caught trout?" teased Howard with barely concealed humour, warming to the subject.

Naida considered the question.

Lowenna's eyes narrowed to slits. "Freshly speared," she added loudly with malevolent undertone.

Marianne froze and gripped the table. She then covered her eyes with her hands.

Ivor squeezed her shoulder. "Lowenna stop this," he stressed, "You're frightening your Mother."

Lowenna stared at Marianne in silent contempt.

Howard glanced from one to the other. "Now don't go upsetting yourself Marianne, we're only having a bit of fun – don't take it so seriously."

Ivor gently coaxed Marianne's hands from her face. Her gaze shot towards Naida, a look of pleading in her eyes. Naida found herself picking up Marianne's vibration. It was as if her eyes were saying, "Help me."

"It's just a game," Naida assured her. "Hey, I can cook trout – grill it or bake it with lots of tasty seasoning." She didn't consider herself an expert, but made light of it.

"Hmm," Lowenna shrugged dismissively, "That's hardly an answer."

"Stop badgering her," scolded Ivor.

Naida gave a short laugh. "Don't worry – I can take it." Despite her nonchalant attitude, anger began to boil inside her. She tried to think of something smart to say to wipe the smile off their faces. Instead, much to her annoyance found herself biting back tears of frustration – not entirely for herself, but more for Lowennas disrespectful treatment of her Mother. It was as if the girl was tampering with Marianne's mind. Naida construed it sinister.

As for her own behaviour, every time she saw Howard, Naida fluctuated between being inebriated and a half-wit. Whatever was the matter with her, allowing him to affect her this way? She could almost hear her Mother whisper in her ear, "Don't be so emotional Naida; you're usually such a self confident girl."

Howard untangled himself from Lowenna. "Enough!" he said, "This is foolish conversation."

"Don't stop on my account," Naida retorted curtly.

Tom, who had been tucking into his meal with great enthusiasm throughout the exchange of words, now put down his knife and fork. He leaned back in his chair and patted his stomach. "I'm full – couldn't eat another morsel – good meal boy," he said, and then turned to Marianne. "You alright girl – you 'aven't said much. Bit too tiring for you, all this – is it?"

"The evenings running away with the hours," she replied, with a vacant expression.

"C'mon my darlin' – lets take a stroll in the garden, the air's good." Tom took Marianne's hand. "You're cold as winter and it be close this evening."

Howard got up and took his jacket from the hook. "Put this round your shoulders Marianne and go and count the stars."

It was plain Howard had great affection for the Tregartha's. Naida observed how considerate he behaved towards Marianne. Was this the man who had chided her so mercilessly? He puzzled her with his contradictory behaviour. She made an effort to be congenial.

"You have a beautiful home Howard," she acknowledged.

"I am lucky," he answered, "I look forward to returning after a trip. A lot of work was done on the cottage last year – various improvements and now it's fully weather proof in winter. I've kept the original inglenook fireplace."

"Imagine waking up to the sound of the sea," Naida said wistfully. "And it must be a wonderful way to cure insomnia."

"My family have lived at Tamarose for generations. Whole families were born here, living out their lives and dying here and I have no wish to break the chain." He looked serious, as if nothing could be more important.

Ivor chuckled. "Well, let's hope your future wife agrees."

"Oh, she will," he said convincingly, then added, "you know how deeply superstitious the villagers were long ago and of course, a lot still are."

"Yes, that's true," agreed Ivor.

"Well, it's said an old woman called Lilith, the witch who lived up on the hill at Gunwalloe fishing cove, would charge the fishermen a sixpence, a lot in those days, to promise a fair wind."

"I've heard the story," said Ivor, "but there's no bribing the weather gods these days."

"That maybe so Ivor, but the story goes that my ancestor, Henry Elliot, was in love with the beautiful witch and when he died at sea, she was said to be heartbroken for all the children she would never bear and cast a spell, blessing all the men in the Elliot line, wishing happiness for them in their choice of wives, for generations to come."

"That's right, she was a white witch and much loved," said Ivor." What her fate was has never been recorded,"

"The legend says that she disappeared without trace," said Howard. "Maybe she still haunts the seas. There was a lot of strange goings on in those days, and she would have been loathed by the secret orders of darkness."

"They say, in remote places and dense forests it still goes on," Naida said earnestly. "It doesn't bear thinking about."

The men made no comment. Naida fancied they looked guarded.

"It is possible," reflected Naida. Then breaking the tension, went on. "But light always triumphs over darkness, and I'm sure your Lilith outwitted them all."

Lowenna yawned, apparently bored. "I'm going to find Mother and Grandpa," she said hastily.

Naida had forgotten Lowenna was there, so unusually still she had sat.

"So, Howard," continued Naida, "are you saying that each wife would fall in love, not only with the Elliot man, but also with the cottage?"

"Yes and the spell has worked so far," answered Howard.

Ivor laughed, "I wouldn't believe all that superstitious nonsense."

50

"You may mock Ivor, but stranger things have happened," replied Howard." My family held the sea in awe. They lived out of the sea and for the sea. Their way of life endured for centuries."

"It must be strange being the last in the line," mused Naida. She had never met a man who spoke so hypnotically. Her opinion of him was rising.

"It's not strange. It gives me a sense of belonging, and I'm sure I won't be the last of the Elliott's," Howard said lazily, holding her gaze. "I aim to continue the line."

She felt her colour rise and averted her eyes. It was all too easy to lose her sense of reality. She couldn't fathom what the meaning behind his words was, and wondered if perhaps he already had someone in mind to fulfil his fantasy. Someone who understood him.

Chapter 5

Howard rose and stretched his lean muscular body. Taking the onyx lighter from the table, he leant across and lit some candles. They had been sitting in the half dark. "I prefer candlelight on evenings like this," he said, snapping the lighter shut.

Naida smiled. "Yes so do." Beneath his tough exterior he could be quite charming, she acknowledged.

Ivor had wandered off into the garden to join the others. Naida relaxed in her chair. The good food and wine had put her at ease. If this had been a date, the scene was now set for seduction, she imagined.

Howard was looking at her as if she was the most desirable woman had ever laid eyes upon. Her smooth golden skin had a luminous glow in the flicker of the candlelight. Perhaps he had been wrong in his assumptions of her. He was impressed how genuinely fond of her the Tregartha's were and she of them. He watched her with a growing awakening deep in the chore of his being.

The silence was comfortable between them. She raised her eyes to meet his. He saw they were greenish brown, full of strange lights, extremely compelling. She was simply beautiful. There was no other way he could describe her, except perhaps, elusive – different to any other girl he had ever met. Her hair drawn back from her face, gave her fine bone structure a delicate quality – an untouchable

Greek Goddess, he mused. He wanted to unwind it, set it free, cascading, rippling, like an extension of sea. The thought triggered his subconscious. A flash of de ja vu. It was her – the girl of his dream. An icy chill swept through him. It dawned on him that she would face danger and he would be powerless to prevent it.

Naida sensed his reaction and opened her eyes wide, her lips slightly apart.

Howard reached for her hand and said earnestly, "I have enjoyed this evening. I hope you have too."

Naida was not prepared for the electricity that shot between them as their fingertips came into contact. She trembled, her voice was shaky as she said, "I have - yes."

He held her hand securely. "Look," he said in a low voice, "before the others comeback – can I see you again?"

His magnetic stare drew her in. An inner sense signalled alarm. "I don't know," she managed weakly.

. The back door opened, footsteps crossed the kitchen floor.

"I'll take you sightseeing one day in the week – perhaps Gunwalloe," Howard whispered quickly, as if it was a conspiracy. He squeezed her hand tighter. "Okay? I'll pick you up Wednesday morning - ten o'clock."

The others were approaching the door, their voices light and thin. Howard waited agreement.

Naida attempted to retrieve her hand without success. Then heard herself say, "Yes –I'll be ready."

Later Naida wondered if she had made the right decision. At the time she had been in a state of confusion. Her date with Howard had been arranged so hastily. When she mentioned her intentions to Ivor and requested the Wednesday for her day off, he was delighted. "You cannot hope for a better guide. Howard knows everything there is to know about Cornwall." Whatever misgivings she had about going, she thought this was probably true. She was waiting for him with a mixture of apprehension and excitement. Having showered and dressed in a peach coloured shorts suit, her hair fixed in a high pony tail. He arrived early.

"Hi there," he greeted her, "ready?"

"Yes I'm all set," she answered and grabbed her bag. Any nervousness was quickly dispelled by his wide smile. Gone was the earnest mood of their last encounter.

"Don't forget your swimsuit," he said.

She pointed to her canvas bag. "My towel's in here. I'm all prepared."

"Good. We'll drive to Gunwalloe. I can show you Church Cove."

Sitting beside him in the car, Naida was aware of a new dimension to their relationship. The atmosphere between them had changed from the former defensive hostility, to a more relaxed companionship.

Turning right after Culdrose airfield, Howard commented, "The little church which the cove is named after is built into the rock on the north side.

There's a sandy beach and it's a good place to swim."

The car park was nearby. Howard led Naida across the sand. With a wide sweep of has hand he gestured across the expanse.

"This is the place where my ancestor, Henry Elliot, buried his vast hoard of treasure. Ships were wrecked on these rocks."

Naida could visualize this distant sea rover and wondered if Howard had inherited his buccaneer spirit. "Really?" she said, "Can you imagine it happening today?"

"Sometimes when I come here out of holiday season and the beach is empty – yes – I can almost feel a presence," murmured Howard, his gaze fixed on the horizon.

"I can understand that," Naida agreed solemnly.

He glanced at her. "Do you know?" he said brightly, as if to lighten the mood. "Legend has it that if a dark haired maiden sits on yonder Croony rock, gazing out to sea for long enough, on the eve of Samhain Pagan festival, her true love will come over the horizon on a sailing ship." His eyes twinkled. He gave a deep throaty laugh, bringing Naida back to the present.

"You and your legends Howard! But somehow I have the feeling this one is true." She ran off across the sand laughing back at him and found a spot to place their towels. Stripping off her shorts-suit to reveal a skimpy leopard print bikini, she ran towards the sea. "Race you to the water," she yelled.

"I told you- you're a mermaid," he shouted after her.

She was too quick for him. Waist deep she dived in and swam out to Croony rock. Before she could reach it, Howard came up behind her. He grabbed her around the waist.

"Caught you." His strong arms turned her around to face him. The close contact his firm body against her skin sent shivers down her spine.

"Let go Howard – I want to reach the rock." She struggled free, Disconcerted by the pleasure she was feeling in his arms.

He dived beneath the waves and pulled her under. She surfaced and saw him laughing.

"That was a dirty trick," she gulped and made again for the rock.

"It's no good swimming to Croony rock. The spell only works on the eve of Samhain," he shouted above the roar of the sea.

"I'm not interested in finding my true love today," she called back.

"Is that so?" he swum up beside her and grabbed hold of her playfully again.

This time she had no wish to free herself and did not resist as his lips brushed against her forehead. One hand encircling her waist, he traced her spine up to the nape of her neck. Their eyes locked and before she realised what was happening, his lips found hers. The effect it had on her emotions astonished her. She felt a rush of excitement. He felt her response with unexpected surprise.

"Well, well, my little mermaid has feelings for me after all," he breathed.

She wrenched herself free, suddenly aware of the implications. Don't kid yourself," she retorted.

"You had few hang-ups that night of the barbecue. If you remember I had to put you to bed," he teased.

Naida's discomfiture was obvious. "What did happen?" she asked warily.

"You mean to tell me you've forgotten!" he replied with amusement.

She sent him a querulous glance; sure he was winding her up. "There was nothing to forget," she snapped.

He held her gaze tauntingly. "Did it mean that little to you? What a travesty," he teased with mock outrage, he then gave a wry smile. "Don't worry, I'm only kidding. It's not my style to take advantage. I assure you, I am, as always, never less than a gentleman."

Not wanting to pursue the subject further, she pushed him away. He swam to the shore and went to dry off in the sun. He watched her firm sinuous body emerge slowly from the water and walk gracefully up the beach towards him.

"How can anyone look so good with wet hair?" he murmured as she drew close.

This tempted her to flick it over him playfully.

"Naida," he chided and pulled her down onto the towel. She fell in a heap against him.

Moving quickly to her own towel she patted the droplets of water from her body. He leant over and proceeded to apply her suntan oil with light sensuous strokes. She conceded it would be churlish to refuse. The expertise of his fingertips massaged her into submission.

"That feels good," she purred lazily.

"Ah, Naida, Naida," her name slipped tantalizingly from his lips, "mysterious and beautiful. I know what it means."

She lay on her stomach, her head to one side. "You've studied Greek mythology then?"

"I have – and it's the perfect name for you. The Naides are water nymphs – minor deities."

She felt his breath warm on her back and her voice quivered. "Yes –rivers and lakes are their territory."

Gently he rolled her over onto her back and began stroking the soothing oil along her arm. She wondered whether he was aware of the arousing affect he was having upon her. She closed her eyes, she could hardly speak. As he leant over her, his hands resting either side of her, she opened her eyes into his.

"Their favours were sought with gifts of honey, flowers and produce of the countryside," he murmured huskily.

She sat up and reached for the bottle of oil, forcing him to move. She managed to find her voice again. "Thanks, I'll finish this now."

He rolled over onto his towel and stretched out languidly. She applied the oil to the rest of her body, and then laid back to soak up the sun.

Once Naida had rationalized her muddled thoughts, she sat up and looked down at Howard. Apparently he was sleeping, one knee raised, one arm across his face. She unfastened the picnic hamper Mrs Dunn had prepared, and placed the food onto the cloth. Howard stirred, opened his eyes and leant up on his elbow.

"You beauty!" he exclaimed, "I'm starving."

The food and drink revived them as they sat looking out to sea.

"Where do you fish from?" asked Naida

"Up there at the fishing cove." Howard pointed in the direction." We can take a walk if you like and I'll show you."

"Okay, and then you can tell me all about your ancestors."

As they strolled slowly along the waters edge, Naida listened with interest to Howard.

"My Grandfathers life up until the late nineteen forties was overseen by the tides – entwined in the rhythms of nature. The fishermen would follow the fish."

"You mean they were closer to nature compared to the men in the city?" asked Naida, "I suppose a sixth sense was in their genes."

"Yes, the sea held a mystical quality for the fishermen. They were deeply religious, calling, in the name of the Lord, each time they cast their nets. They suffered great hardships." Howard shook his head, "and they still considered themselves fortunate – extraordinary."

Naida noticed how his hair had dried into springy, untamed coils at the nape of his neck. A primeval savage, she fancied. A pirate!

"You know," he continued, "they took to sea sometimes at two a.m. reliant on the changeable tides – for weeks on end, huddled in their oilskins hauling in the fish."

Naida grimaced. "It certainly was a hard life."

"It was. The boats were primitive and the men slept on narrow wooden bunks."

This disillusioned Naida's whimsical thread of thought. "It sounds horrendous. How uncomfortable," she observed. "They must have had great courage."

"They did. The trips were rarely achieved without loss of life. Sunday was a taboo day for fishing; they would always pull into the nearest port. Women had all the dirty work on shore."

Any romantic fantasies she had left were dampened. "That's typical. Men haven't changed that much then have they?" she laughed and watched his reaction.

He raised an eyebrow and acknowledged her words with a short laugh. "They never allowed women onboard the boats because it was considered unlucky by the men. But the women ran the town!"

"That's good!" exclaimed Naida. Her intuition told her he liked to be in control. She had just escaped from a household of domineering men and wasn't looking for another.

"It's different nowadays. Strict supervision regulates every aspect from guarding the stocks to the size of the nets." He stooped to pick up a pebble and aimed it at the sea.

No, she was wrong; he wasn't like any man from her family. He respected life. "It makes you realise how nothing ever stays the same," she said.

"What do you mean?" he asked.

She stood beside him and watched the waves break on the shore. "The only thing we can be sure of is change."

"That's true. When you think how man has progressed in such a short time," he said.

"In our Great Grandparents time they never had aeroplanes let alone rockets landing on the moon," she said. "Incredible!"

"Some progress is good, some is not," he stated. "If mans intellect goes too far with technology, overriding his spirituality…," he shrugged.

"It scares me wondering where it will all lead," Naida looked up into the sky. The sun played chase with a stray cloud and won. She blinked. "But these are extraordinary times we live in."

The echoes that haunted her from the past quietened in her soul. It was all so fascinating. A new peace moved through her spirit. Howard's thoughts were so profound they matched hers. Seagulls squawked overhead and flew gracefully to the rocks, observing the human intruders with a common bond. Naida recalled an old Red Indian saying she once heard; 'the earth and I are of one mind. The measure of the land and the measure of our bodies are the same.'

Old Moorstone farm was quiet early evening as they drove up. Howard and Naida got out of the car.

"I must be getting back now," said Howard, "I've got a few things to catch up on. How about coming to dinner at my place tomorrow night?" He took her hand in his and inclined his head towards her. Naida was sure he was about to kiss her, when they were interrupted.

"Hey Howard, where have you been?" called Lowenna. It was almost an accusation. Naida didn't know whether to be disappointed or relieved. Lowenna glared furiously at them both.

"There's no need to look like that Lowenna. We've been swimming!" said Howard in surprise.

"Swimming!" she repeated. "Well what about me? You told me you would take me in the holidays."

"I said if I have the time." He was beginning to feel irritated.

"You seem to have plenty of time for her," Lowenna scowled at their linked hands, turned on her heels and stalked indoors.

Howard shook his head and sighed. "Don't take any notice of our Lowenna. She can be a precocious child at times."

"Child? I wouldn't call her that and she seems very attached to you," observed Naida.

"I suppose she is a little possessive. Being an only child she sees me as her older brother." He was torn between excusing Lowenna and placating Naida. "Oh forget it. Now, dinner tomorrow night?" he pleaded.

Naida hesitated. She didn't want to entangle him in her problems. The last thing she intended was to place him in danger. She would have to resolve her past and come clean before she became too involved with him. Her head told her she must refuse his invite, but his earnest gaze would not leave her and her heart overruled.

62

"Yes," she whispered. "Tomorrow night."

The evening passed without incident. After small talk over dinner Naida decided to catch up on her art work. Lowenna had sulked throughout the meal and later went into the village to meet some friends. Naida was determined to ignore the younger girl's moods.

Chapter 6

The following evening Naida borrowed the land rover and drove into the village. The stark white silhouette of Howard's cottage lit the landscape in the evening sun, like a beacon guiding her in. An unknown force beyond her control urged her on, compelling her to meet him tonight. As he opened the door it struck her how handsome he looked. Metallic blue eyes shone out in contrast from his deeply tanned face.

"Hello beautiful lady," he greeted her.

Words stuck in her throat. She managed to collect herself. "Hi Howard, something smells delicious."

"I'm flattered. Do you mean me or the meal?" he teased.

She gave him a wry smile. "Both I hope. This sea air gives me an appetite."

"Your wish is my command mon cherie. I will serve you my nouvelle cuisine. Non? Oui?"

Not a very good French accent, thought Naida with amusement. "Oui. I cannot wait Monsieur."

"Take a seat by the window Mademoiselle." He pulled out her chair and bowed extravagantly.

After the delicious meal he led her to the sofa to finish their wine. He gazed thoughtfully into the red liquid, swilling it gently around the glass.

"I dreamt of you one night, before we met," he confided. "You walked into the sea and an enormous shark devoured you." He pulled a mock horror face. "I couldn't reach you – and then you were gone." He looked serious for a moment and then smiled softly. "You truly are the girl of my dreams."

Naida shivered. "Do you believe in ghosts, Howard?"

"I believe some people are aware of the supernatural. Some have the gift of second sight. You can't help but believe when working and living close to nature as I do," he paused, and then continued. "There are many things we cannot understand with our mere mortal minds."

"I think ghosts are earthbound spirits too attached to the earth to travel on to other spheres," she surmised and then added, "They are sad souls."

"That's feasible," he agreed, "but we cannot say for sure – it is not so clear cut. Sometimes they could be an imprint on the ether caused by some dramatic event. Could not some so called ghosts come down from the higher spheres to help?"

"To help their loved ones on earth, yes." This idea appealed to Naida. She was curious. "Have you ever experienced anything unusual?"

"When I was at sea I saw a mermaid perched on a rock, like a drowned rat with green eyes." He glanced sideways at her, managing to keep a straight face.

"Oh – don't be so stupid," she chided.

"No, seriously, I was once caught in a storm out at sea. I swear Henry Elliot and Lilith appeared to me. Of course I could have been hallucinating. The wind and waves lashing over the boat were ferocious. It was wild, but shortly afterwards the storm subsided."

Naida looked pensively out through the open window to the darkening sky. She said in a hushed voice. "Once, on a warm summer's night when it was still and silent - I remember it happened in Cyprus when everything was in tune. I sat alone and looked up to the planets and stars. I felt I was a tiny speck in the vast universe. I knew then there is so much more to experience we will come to know." She caught his intense gaze and stopped. He would think her ludicrous.

"Go on," he urged, fascinated. He was not ridiculing her.

This encouraged her to continue. "It was strange. I could feel myself floating up through imaginary clouds. I was focused on a shining silver star, the Stella Polaris. If I had let go I'm sure I could have reached it. A great ocean of life out there, hiding secrets…" She hesitated and lowered her eyes,

He observed her, mesmerised, positive he would drown in the depths of her large eyes – full of starlight and emeralds. "You are a witch Naida. You have certainly cast a spell on me – Aphrodite of the sea."

"Tell me about Lilith the white witch. Was she ever happy?" Naida wondered swiftly. He was churning up her emotions again.

"Yes, I'm sure she found happiness. She had inner strength. After all, she was like you I believe – a visionary. Or are you just a daydreamer?" He mulled this over, and then continued. "She was a seer. Although she lost her Henry, his memory was part of her soul. She devoted the rest of her life to the people of the village."

"She sounds a special person." Naida was satisfied.

"Infact I have a book of ancient Celtic prose, said to be written by Lilith. It was handed down to me from my Father."

"Have you?" enthused Naida, "I would love to see it."

He went in search of it and returned with an old, dusty brown book. "Here it is." He leafed through the pages. "Ah, talking about my dream, here's one called Dream Time." He went on in a low voice. *"Scattered images in humble dreams seem insignificant until interpreted in symbolic state and awareness dawns. Generations of ritual occur before me, custodians of a sacred land."*

"Let me see," Naida glanced at the page, and then carried on reading. *"I catch a glimpse of perfect love and life beyond the stars, transported to some distant place, where parted lovers weep no more, foretelling sometime future days, vivid messages within the mind."* She stopped for a moment wide eyed, and then said, "I used to write my dreams down, otherwise they just disappear into the ether and I never can remember them."

The subtle light from the candle flickered dimly across the page. He looked at her and the flame within his own heart scorched the air between them. With burning desire he drew her to him. Before she could think rationally his lips were on hers, with an intensity she had never experienced before. She tried to resist, and then gave up, quivering with emotion as his fingers slowly traced her cheek and caressed her face, gently rippling down her neck.

She could hardly bear the delicious sensations rising from deep within her.

"Naida lets reach those heights together. Let me take you to another dimension," he murmured.

She fought fiercely against her desire, knowing she could not give herself freely. Love making was too sacred to be taken lightly. Would it mean more to her than him? She could not allow herself to fall in love with him. Too many secrets stood between them. No, it was impossible. Her passion intensified dangerously. With great effort she broke away from his embrace and cried, "Howard, no!"

"Sweetheart what are you afraid of? What are you running away from?"

The hurt on his face was more than she could endure. She stood up. "It's late Howard, I must go."

She flew out of the door and into the land rover before he could stop her. Her hands were shaking on the steering wheel. Her thoughts were in turmoil.

Later, she was silently thankful that she had arrived back safely. The state she was in she could hardly remember the drive back at all.

She slept fitfully that night and dreamt of her Mother and Lilith, standing outside a house. She tried to look out of the window but her eyes would not focus. Voices were calling her to open the door. She had the sensation of being an actor in a film and all the while in the background a small boy played merrily on a flute.

She awoke in a sweat, the memory of the dream still vivid. What could it mean? Sitting up, she noticed the poetry book beside her bed. She must have taken it in her haste. She had been clutching it when Howard had kissed her. Drawn towards it, she opened the pages at random and read; "*Lonely heart, I behold you in your house of glass from the outside looking in, struggling to survive within the mirror of your mind. Young lovers divided by the sea, reduced to wailing tears. Lonely heart I know you well, wistful face at the window, mouthing words without sound. How I long to break the glass and set you free.*"

Naida dropped the book onto the bed with a sense of foreboding.

Chapter 7

For the next few days, Naida threw herself into her work. There was plenty to keep her busy. Howard did not call, which caused Lowenna to remark at breakfast: "Howard had enough of you, has he Naida? Looks like he's avoiding you."

"No. I've been too busy to see him," Naida answered in a matter of fact voice, almost convincing herself.

"He gets bored. His girlfriends are usually short term, I saw him yesterday. He's taking me swimming on Sunday." She gloated triumphant and bit into her toast.

"Good. You'll enjoy that." Naida was curt. "Now if you'll excuse me I have work to do." She got up having no wish to endure another moment of Lowenna's company.

The following week went by with no word from Howard. Naida tried to push thoughts of him to the back of her mind. However, Lowenna had other ideas and gave her a detailed account of their swimming trip, and then sat with a smug, self satisfied smile on her face.

"Let them do as they please," Naida told Tom later. "I'm really not interested," answering Tom's concerned enquiry as to why she had not seen Howard lately.

As the days went by, Naida managed, by sheer willpower, to deaden all her feelings for Howard. She directed all her energies into helping Ivor at the smallholding and congratulated herself on how well she was doing.

One particularly bright afternoon, Ivor asked her if she would pick up some fruit from the orchard. Her mood was carefree. The sun was hot, but not stifling and a gentle breeze, coming from the sea, caressed her limbs. She filled the basket with fallen pears and went to the far end of the orchard to sit on the gate to rest. Closing her eyes she breathed in the fragrant air. Nothing could spoil this day, not even Howard's absence.

Unfortunately the wheel of life moves in unexpected ways and had lulled her into false security. Before she had time to let out her breath, a hand roughly grabbed hold of her shoulder and another hand was clapped over her mouth. Too shocked to scream, even if she could, she found herself looking into two cold black eyes.

"Got you," he snapped. Petros, who was always a devious child, had grown into an arrogant man. "If you promise not to yell, I'll let you go."

She nodded reluctantly. He may well be her stepbrother, but there was certainly no love lost between them. "How did you find me?" she gasped.

"It wasn't difficult. Your outstanding good looks did not go unnoticed." A cruel twist curved his mouth. "The ticket officer at the station was most helpful. You should have been more careful about covering your tracks."

Naida wished she had not stopped to ask directions. "Damn you Petros. Just go home and leave me alone."

He dug his fingers into her shoulder. "No way! You are coming back with me where you belong. Your marriage has been arranged and you will not bring dishonour on the family."

She struggled angrily. "Dishonour! What rubbish. For God's sake Petros, we were both brought up in England."

He shrugged. "Father made a good deal with Rico Pettroulli. You will be a wealthy woman and none of us will want for anything ever again."

Naida could hardly believe what she was hearing. Rico Pettroulli was an old man, a friend of her stepfathers. He was a lecherous old widower. She felt sick to her stomach.

"Never!" she screamed at him.

In her repulsion and fear, she tore herself away from his grasp and ran like one demented, up the path to the waiting land rover. She fumbled for the spare set of keys in her pocket and started the engine. Heading instinctively towards the village, she caught sight of Petros car in the mirror.

Reaching Mrs Dunn's cottage, she screeched to a halt, jumped out and ran to the door, which was opened by a very surprised Mrs Dunn, awakened from her afternoon nap by the frantic knocking.

"Whatever is the matter m' dear?" she enquired with great concern at the shaking girl standing before her.

"Please can I come in?" Naida managed to gasp. "Thank goodness you're home."

"Of course dear, of course."

Naida hurriedly shut the door behind her. "Someone was following me," she said in explanation.

"Oh Naida, you 'ad better be careful. There's been talk of a strange man in the village trying to entice girls into his car – a flasher they said."

"Err – oh there is?" She knew even Petros would not stoop to this.

"I think you should call the police."

"No – no," stammered Naida. "I'm alright now Mrs Dunn. He's gone anyway – could be miles away by now."

"Well, if you say so." Mrs Dunn was uneasy. Naida was in obvious distress. "What colour car was it?"

"Um – red I think."

"Oh well, the one they've been talking about is dark blue." She relaxed a little. "I'll make us a nice cup of tea."

Lowenna, who happened to be passing through the village, witnessed the last part of the drama with great interest. Hidden from view, she watched Naida's flight in the land rover followed by Petros hot pursuit. Obviously Naida knew the man. Whatever was going on she was determined to find out.

By the time she was ready to leave Naida had calmed down. She begged Mrs Dunn not to worry the Tregartha's with the events of this afternoon. She assured her she would be alright and drove off.

Ivor was waiting at the door looking perplexed. "Naida where have you been? I found the basket of pears by the gate and the land rover gone. I was waiting for you to bring them to the shed."

"I'm sorry Ivor. I went into the village and was longer than I meant to be. I was going to bring them afterwards." She had completely forgotten. "I hope I'm not too late."

"No it's alright. I was just worried about you," he sounded concerned. "I expect you've heard about these rumours circulating in the village."

Naida swallowed. "Yes. Don't worry about me. I can take care of myself."

"As long as you're okay. Do be careful though."

The incident left Naida withdrawn. Fear kept her close to the farm. Extra vigilance was called for when she went about her daily work. Hours slid by into days, long and drawn out. Darkness came late as the sun refused to sleep. Most evenings Naida sat outside under the big elm tree, watching the clouds progress around the setting sun, forming shapes in the pink night sky. She collected her thoughts racing erratically through her mind, attempting to put things in perspective.

She existed in a sort of limbo. Sooner or later she would have to meet her problems head on. Or was it herself she had to face first? Unconsciously she feared the consequences. It was as if by setting the proceedings in motion, she had committed the crime of opening old wounds that were perhaps left alone. If only her Mother was still alive, she would know what to do. But it was precisely because she wasn't that Naida was here in this predicament now. She could almost here her mother saying, "Don't be so hard on yourself, kori."

Living with this self inflicted guilt forced her to work harder and harder, pushing herself in some sort of imagined penance, until her muscles ached from sheer exhaustion. By the end of the week she looked fit to drop, which did not go unnoticed.

At dinner that evening Ivor commented, "Naida, you've been working so hard, I think you deserve a treat." He paused and lay back in his chair. "I've arranged with Howard for you to go scuba diving with him and Lowenna at the weekend."

Naida looked up from her plate. "Oh – I don't think…" she started to protest.

"You deserve a break from this boring routine. We won't have you being a Cinderella any more," continued Ivor. "You said yourself you would love the chance to scuba dive. I haven't seen you go to the beach lately. You're missing all this lovely weather."

Naida was touched by his kindness and it was true, scuba diving was too good to miss.

"How do Howard and Lowenna feel about this?" she asked.

Tom shot a glance at Ivor, who straightened and said. "They will be pleased to show you the ropes."

Naida realised she may not get the opportunity again. "In that case, okay, I'll go," she answered with slight reservations.

Saturday morning started with a mixture of sunshine and showers. Grey clouds scurried by, eventually breaking up to reveal a rainbow of myriad colours, reaching from Old Moorstone Farm down to the sea. This cast doubts on the days plans.

But to everyone's relief the sky cleared to the boundless blue they had come to rely on.

Whatever Lowenna's opinion of including Naida on their trip, on all accounts she appeared to show no malice. Howard on the other hand behaved indifferent towards her, as if nothing had happened between them and was preoccupied with the task of seeing to the safety of the divers.

The boat was anchored by the entrance to a cave beneath jutting rock, reached by a steep cliff path. Another boat came alongside, parallel. Howard spoke to the man on board, whilst Lowenna and Naida went below to don their suits. Naida appeared on deck first, leaving Lowenna to sort out the diving gear.

Howard beckoned her over. "Naida, this is a friend of mine, Blake. He will be diving in about an hour, in search of a sunken vessel and wondered if anyone would like to join him."

She turned to Blake with interest. "Hi there, have you reason to believe there is one down there?"

He nodded, "More than likely Miss – there's a rumour."

"If the others are diving you can count me in," she enthused.

"If we're back in time," said Howard. "First I want to take you through the cave to become accustomed to the depths."

Lowenna brought the diving cylinders over and they fastened the regulators.

"Right then. Stay close behind me Naida," advised Howard. He turned to Lowenna and informed her of their plans.

"That's fine by me. Let's get going." Lowenna sounded impatient.

Howard lowered himself into the sea first and the girls followed. They entered the water filled cave, passing by a variety of fish. Naida was in her element. Deeper and deeper the graceful trio descended and out the other end of the cave. Later Lowenna signalled that she'd had enough. Howard nodded, knowing she was capable of returning by herself.

Naida swooped down to retrieve a piece of coral, moving with the rhythm of the sea. Howard swam around to face her, pointing out an exotic shoal of fish, dancing by in sequence.

Time past all too quickly for Naida. Howard finally pointed to the back entrance of the cave and with a wicked gleam in his eye, motioned for her to race him back.

Naida glided swiftly through the cave. She surfaced out of the entrance ahead of Howard and waited for him to appear. He emerged a few seconds later. She made for the boat. He overtook her, hauled himself up and held out his hands, his eyes fixed softly on her. His earlier indifference seemingly forgotten. Lowenna and Blake were nowhere to be seen.

"Grab hold," he urged. "Sit down and get your breath back."

Hesitantly she did as he asked, keeping her distance.

"I won't bite," he said gently, searching her face. "What is wrong Naida?"

She lowered her eyes, "Nothing Howard," she replied evasively.

"No?" he challenged, "Then why did you leave in such a hurry that night? At least you owe me an explanation. You puzzle me Naida. Can you deny your feelings for me?" He moved closer, his hand brushing her cheek. She knew what he was about to do next.

In the crevices of her mind an alarm sounded. She had not bargained for him to compromise her. Where the hell was Lowenna? For once she wished the girl was here. This was not on the agenda today; she reasoned and turned her head away from him.

"Don't Howard." She kept her head averted so he couldn't see her tremulous expression.

"The more I got to know you I could feel this deep connection growing between us. I have never before felt this way with anyone. I cannot believe you feel nothing for me Naida," he said, "Look me in the eyes and say it."

She could not look at him. "I feel – nothing but friendship for you," she stated flatly, fixing her gaze on their reflections in the water.

"Is there someone else who holds your heart?" he persisted.

"That's none of your business," she replied, her old spark ignited. "In any case you have been dating Lowenna."

He raised his eyebrows quizzically. "You surely don't believe we've been dating," he answered. "She accompanies me sometimes, that's all."

The silence hung leaden in the atmosphere between them. There seemed nothing more to say. Minutes ticked by that seemed like hours. Howard spoke first.

"Look, I haven't brought you here to argue. I respect your honesty."

He was offering an olive branch and she tried to resolve the situation without too much pain.

"Howard," she said slowly, searching for the right words. "I don't want you to get the wrong impression, but I'm just not ready for a serious relationship. I want to enjoy my freedom a little longer," she half lied.

He looked defeated. "Okay, let's call a truce. It will be difficult for me just to be your friend, but if that's what you want, that's what I will offer you. At least that way I shall still have your company."

She bit her lip, her heart heavy. "Thanks for being so understanding."

"We'll say no more about it," he replied. "Now, where has Lowenna got to? It seems she's too impatient to wait for us and must have gone with Blake."

"They will be gone for ages won't they?" said Naida apprehensively. She was beginning to wish she had declined today's treat.

Howard stood up. "Don't worry about being alone with me. I'm not going to jump on you," he mocked. "I'm hungry. How about we get dressed and I'll take you for a purely platonic lunch."

Chapter 8

Angry clouds came suddenly early evening, blocking out the sun, hastening the night prematurely. Thunder rumbled like a door slamming in the sky, which eventually swung wide. Rain poured onto the pavements, washing the dusty, sun parched walls. Streams filled to overflowing. Holiday makers, who had been enjoying the late sunshine, hurriedly folded their deckchairs and ran for cover.

By morning the storm had ceased. The sun shone brilliantly once more with an almost mountain freshness. Naida sighed. Her day spent with Howard yesterday was tinged with regret. In normal circumstances they could have fallen in love like any other couple and let their relationship develop naturally. As it was, she could not lure him into the labyrinth of her problems. She could not live with the consequences. At least they would remain friends, which was some consolation. Despite his apparent acceptance, she decided it would be easier for them both if they saw as little of each other as possible.

This did not prove too difficult. Howard took to scuba diving with a vengeance. His enthusiasm was indomitable and Naida wondered if it had anything to do with her. He seemed to be channelling all his energies into searching for a sunken vessel with Blake. As far as Naida knew, nothing yet had been discovered.

Everybody went about their separate activities. Lowenna was never in. Naida wondered where the girl disappeared to. Ivor was often heard to say. "Where are you off to Lowenna? And can't you wear something more respectable – and don't be late." Lowenna just wafted out in a cloud of musky perfume, sighing impatiently," Yes Father, no Father." She rolled her eyes. "See you later."

Petros had not contacted Naida again. This she took as a good sign that he had returned home. This evening Naida had driven to Gunwalloe to take one of her many walks with Fenn. She was out later than usual and had wandered further. She came across a hidden cove. Dusk began to creep over the horizon.

Fenn bounded along the path. A seagull squawked, flying low overhead. Fenn barked and chased on down around the cliff edge. Ignoring Naida's frantic call, he ran along the cliff face and disappeared behind a secluded rock. Naida followed, fearing for his safety, knowing he would not respond to her call. The seagull was of far more interest. Somehow Fenn had wedged himself onto a small ledge above a sheer drop to the sea. When he saw Naida he whimpered.

"You naughty dog, how on earth did you manage to get...?" She stopped and peered down to the rocky sea below. Someone was diving from a low rock.

There was no mistaking the tawny hair and tanned, broad shoulders. It was Howard. What was he doing down there at this time? She watched him adjust his snorkel and dive in.

The glow from the receding sun had gone now. Clouds were gathering. Darkness was rapidly obscuring the view. Naida stood against the breeze for a moment and decided she had better get Fenn back to safety, while she could still see.

The light flicked on in the kitchen just as Naida came through the door. "Oh – Marianne!" said Naida in surprise. "I didn't expect to see…."

"You're out late tonight Naida," cut in Marianne quickly.

Naida unclipped Fenn's lead and went to hang it on the hook. "Yes I just took Fenn for a long walk."

Marianne looked unusually calm. Her eyes never left Naida. "I was about to make some hot chocolate. I'm fed up with that herbal drink they always bring me."

"Herbal drink! Who gives you that?" asked Naida.

Marianne did not answer. She walked over to the stove. "The winds dropped, thank goodness. Ivor has gone into the village to pick up Tom from the Fisheries Inn. I was worried we were going to have a storm and they wouldn't get home in time. Would you like some hot chocolate?"

"Err – yes please," replied Naida. She was astonished to find Marianne so coherent.

"I don't like storms," said Marianne, lighting the hob. "Lightening can come through windows and walls. Nothing can stop it. But I still hide when the thunder roars like a lion."

"Well – I don't think…," began Naida, somewhat bemused. "Yes – the storms down here can be quite bad can't they?"

Marianne filled the mugs with her back to Naida. She turned and carried the hot drinks carefully over to the table. "Oh yes," she answered in a whisper, staring intently at Naida.

Naida smiled at her gently. "You know, it's very unlikely to be struck by lightening indoors. It's a million to one chance."

"No – you don't understand – the thunder is looking for me." Marianne seemed utterly convinced.

"What!" replied Naida. "Of course it's not. Whatever gave you that idea?"

"They – they told me."

"Who told you?"

Marianne looked down at her mug. "I liked you from the first time I met you. I recognise something inside you – the light. I...," she trailed off.

"That's kind of you," replied Naida. "I like you too."

"I know I can trust you," said Marianne, wide eyed, and then continued with urgency. "I've got something to tell..."

"Why don't you tell her about Lilith- Mother?"

They both spun round. Lowenna stood in the doorway.

"Oh!" said Naida, startled. "I didn't hear you come in."

"I wasn't out," answered Lowenna. "As it happens I was in my room."

Marianne sat like a statue, ashen faced.

Lowenna turned to Naida. "Did you go out this evening?"

"Yes, I took Fenn for a walk to Gunwalloe."

Lowenna sat down. Although she appeared outwardly calm, Naida sensed a chilling undertone.

"Have you heard the legend of Lilith?" she asked with a smirk.

"Yes, Howard did mention her," replied Naida, wondering what was coming next.

"But I bet he didn't tell you everything – about how she still haunts the cliffs at Gunwalloe," went on Lowenna.

Marianne began to tremble.

Lowenna continued. "Lilith died of a broken heart – some say she was murdered – wasn't she Mother?"

It was as if Marianne had disappeared inside her head. The veil had come down once more.

"Yes it's true you know. Tell her Mother, won't you? Tell her about the spot on the cliff where Lilith has been seen at night. It's not clear if she was pushed over the edge or jumped. The rocks below are jagged but at high tide a body can be swept out and claimed by the sea forever."

"I didn't know she came to such a horrible end." Naida weighed Lowenna up shrewdly.

Lowenna went on with frightening intensity. "The ghost of Lilith returns to the cliffs in search of her lost lover."

"Is that so?" remarked Naida, trying to take all of this in. Was Lowenna trying to scare her?

"If she cannot find him," continued Lowenna, her tone casual now, "It is said that whoever should have the misfortune to encounter her will be lured over the edge."

Naida was aware of Marianne's discomfiture and said. "Oh, these stories get embroidered over the ages. I wonder who made that one up."

84

Lowenna glared at them both. "Maybe she knew too much," she snapped irritably, through pinched lips.

Naida noticed her cold and colourless grey eyes.

"Those who know too much and tell," continued Lowenna with a vindictive edge, "are destroyed."

Marianne stood up awkwardly, almost knocking over her chair. With a short gasp she fled from the room.

"Marianne it's alright – don't listen to her." Naida called after her.

"Leave her – she's just having an attack of nerves. Mother's over sensitive you know," drawled Lowenna, dismissing any concern.

"That's cruel! Why do you upset her with your stories of Lilith if you know she reacts like that?" retorted Naida. Lowenna had done her utmost to be unpleasant.

Lowenna smirked. "It's not how it seems. I try to make her confront her fears. She can't run away from her own shadow forever, can she?" I'm only trying to help her."

Naida could not believe what she was hearing. The girl was deluded. She had a warped mind. "Rubbish! I don't think that's a good way to go about it," she observed.

"Well, it's not your problem, is it? She's my Mother."

Naida sipped the last of her drink and studied Lowennas expressionless face – empty of emotion.

"What did she say to you?" Lowenna asked presently, her eyes narrowing. "She rambles you know – lives in her own imaginary world."

"Actually, she was quite rational I thought, before you came in," said Naida pointedly.

"Hmm!" said Lowenna, her thoughts ticking over. "So – you went to Gunwalloe tonight?" There was displeasure in her tone.

"That's right – I told you," said Naida. This prompted her to remember Howard and it occurred to her that he may be unsafe. The thought of him down there at the mercy of the sea sent shivers through her body.

"I would keep away from there if I were you," warned Lowenna.

"Why? It's a great place to walk," said Naida, and then added carefully, "I even think people dive from the rocks – at night."

"No – you're mistaken," Lowenna said sharply. "You didn't see anyone – did you?"

Naida hesitated. It would not be wise to confide in Lowenna!

"It was too dark to see far below the cliffs," she replied.

Lowenna sat back in her chair and eyed Naida with a trace of scepticism. "I'm going to bed now," she yawned.

Naida sat alone awhile longer; the nagging worry about Howard persisted. Eventually she dragged herself off to bed. Utterly exhausted, she fell into a troubled sleep. She dreamt she was swimming furiously trying to escape. Everywhere she turned, avoiding the weeds that threatened to trap her, she came face to face with herself. There was no escaping.

So terrifying was the nightmare, that her subconscious cut the dream at the point where she met herself once again. She then found herself on the cliff overlooking the cove. The mist was thick late evening. She tried to see the moon clearly, but only a faint outline was visible. All the time she was aware of a figure, clothed in white. She watched the figure levitate and turn to look in her direction. She was looking into the face of an angel, a serene aura surrounding her.

Naida slept the rest of the night peacefully. She was awakened abruptly at dawn, brought back into waking consciousness by Fenn barking. The memory of her dream was still strong. She shivered despite the warmth of the early morning. It was just beginning to get light. She heard whispering outside and then a car sped off. Footsteps came up the stairs and stopped at Lowennas room, and then silence. Nobody else had stirred, which was lucky for Lowenna, thought Naida. The girl must have crept out sometime in the night. Naida sighed and dozed off again.

Chapter 9

The Fisheries Inn, a local haunt of fishermen, farmers and tourists alike, buzzed with speculation amid the chatter and raised voices thronging the bar tonight. A week had past since Naida had first sighted Howard diving late. She had continued to take Fenn for his evening walk along the same route. Not because she might catch a glimpse of Howard, or so she told herself. But sure enough he had been there the same time, the same place every evening.

She had come to the Fisheries Inn with Tom tonight. Occasionally she accompanied him and mingled with the locals. Tom had said she would find the true spirit of Cornwall here in the heart of these men and women. She had not been disappointed. Ever watchful eyes were wary at first, but any friend of the Tregartha's must be alright and she was soon accepted.

Tom came back from the bar with their drinks. "Bin some talk 'bout smugglers, seems like one of the youngsters found some gold bars and that's a fact, hidden 'neath the cliffs at Gunwalloe. Couldn't believe 'is eyes yer know. Two solid gold blocks."

"Do you really think its smugglers?" asked Naida, eyes widening.

"You'd be surprised. But yer know, the fishermen in these parts don't take kindly to it," warned Tom. "So keep it under yer 'at," he winked. "We don't want to fuel any gossip."

"I wonder where they come from." Naida thought aloud.

"Anyone's guess. Then there again it went on last year, but the police couldn't nail 'em and they got clean away with it yer know."

"Could it be the same men – professional smugglers?"

"Shh – we don't want the "Emmett's" to get wind of it. Sightseeing will be rife."

"Who are the Emmett's?" Naida imagined a feudal family.

Tom laughed. "Oh – that's what we locals call the holiday makers."

"I would imagine it would attract the crowds," agreed Naida.

"That's a fact – too true it would and I wouldn't advise you to go strolling late along those cliffs either. Some nasty characters, those smugglers."

"Do you think Howard knows about this?" wondered Naida with alarm.

"I don't know, 'e's said nothing." Tom paused, thoughtful. "More than likely though, 'e knows most things that go on around 'ere."

Naida suspected that Howard's late night diving had been a way of exorcising the memory of her from his heart in the lonely evenings. Never the less he could be in danger. She would have to warn him. Whatever danger Tom had suggested that she herself might encounter, nothing could deter her. She would confront him tomorrow night.

More determined than ever, she set out the following evening. Tom's words echoed in her head. She chose to disregard them. Although she had locked her fears away, she hadn't thrown away the key. By now Fenn knew by habit where they were going and ran on ahead. He stopped behind a narrow cleft of rock and barked. Naida caught up with him quietly and looked in the direction of his eager excitement. She had expected to see Howard once more, but sprang back when she heard voices.

"Shh Fenn," she whispered.

Luckily no-one had heard him, due to his bark being lost in the whistle of the wind. There was no sign of Howard. Naida put Fenn's lead on and stayed hidden.

She could make out the rasping tones of Petros' voice and the harsh words of the smugglers. They were arguing.

"Give me my cut," demanded Petros.

"Not until you've delivered the gold to your contacts in London. When we are paid you shall have you're cut," came the cold reply.

So that is what Petros has been up to, thought Naida. He has obviously been snooping around, gone down to the smugglers and made himself known to them. Then he had offered to make a deal with London's underworld, who would buy the gold. She suspected that he was involved in protection rackets. However, she had never voiced her suspicions as her Mother would have been devastated. He was despicable.

Fenn pulled on the lead, whining with excitement. Naida tugged him back. He struggled violently, slipped out of his collar and ran to the edge. In his urgency he knocked a loose boulder over the cliff. The men looked up.

"What was that? There's someone up there," shouted Petros. "Come on, don't let them get away!"

Naida grabbed Fenn, jammed the collar over his head and ran. She could hear them gain rapidly on her. It was quite dark now and the mist was rising. She went down a few steps and squeezed between two rocks, her hand clenched firmly over Fenn's mouth. She spoke to him gently and he stopped struggling. Whatever happens they must not find her.

"Can you see the bugger?" A voice snapped in the darkness.

"Christ, I can't see my hand in front of my face. We'll not find 'em now."

The men retreated. Naida waited. She then let her breath out. The mist was suffocating. She edged her way out and peered around. She had only gone a few paces when Fenn started to growl, the fur rising on his back. Naida had the uneasy feeling of being observed. Fenn refused to budge. To her horror she could make out a white figure. It reminded her of her dream. She stood rigid. Then as quickly as it had materialised, the figure faded into the mist. An aura of malevolence left over from the smugglers hung in the air. The hidden moon was full. Had her mind been doing tricks again? Ever since she was a child, if she wanted to change something unpleasant, or create beauty all she had to do was attempt to visualize it. Her Stepfather scolded her and Petros jeered, but her Mother always understood. Had she hallucinated in her terror? She pulled on Fenn's lead and fled.

Howard was talking to Ivor and Tom when Naida entered the farmhouse. She ran a hand self-consciously through her dishevelled hair. The wind had arranged it into wild unruly curls. The men looked concerned.

"You're late girl. We were getting worried," said Tom.

"You look like you've seen a ghost," declared Howard.

If you only knew, thought Naida dryly, but said. "Just a bit wind blown, that's all."

"You haven't been up to Gunwalloe this late – on your own?" said Ivor as he stirred his hot drink.

She was surprised at this unexpected reception. "I didn't mean to be so late back. Fenn was so enjoying his run I completely forgot the time"

Tom yawned. "It's past my bedtime." He got up from the kitchen table and turned to Naida. "Take heeds my girl – goodnight."

Ivor drained his cup. "I'm off to bed too. Now Naida's back she can keep you company Howard."

Howard leant forward, resting his hands under his chin. Naida stood opposite. The walls seemed to close in on them. He raised his eyes. They caressed her across the room. She sought desperately for words to keep the atmosphere casual, but failed miserably. Howard spoke first.

"How are things Naida?"

"Oh fine," she answered lightly. "And you?"

"Good – me too," was all he volunteered and then they lapsed into an awkward silence.

Some friendship, thought Naida. She sat down at the table and looked down at her hands. Her knuckles were bleeding. She must have grazed them on the rocks. Swiftly she removed them from the table, but not in time.

Howard dropped his guard. "What have you done to your hand?

Naida rubbed her knuckle, unconcerned. "It's just a graze."

"Let me see." He caught her by the wrist. "How on earth did you do that? I'll get a bandage."

"Don't bother. I'll do it myself," she protested, retracting her wrist from his light grasp.

Unperturbed, he headed for the first aid box. Selecting a length of gauze, he cleansed and dressed her wound. He kept his eyes diligently on her hands as he spoke. "I had a feeling you were in danger tonight. Call it what you like -telepathy?" he shrugged. "What happened Naida? You look drained."

She had a desperate need to confide in him and share her burden. Then she remembered Petros was part of the nightmare and checked herself.

"I – went along the cliff path – quite a long way…" she ventured cautiously.

"Yes?" he encouraged.

She took a deep breath and plunged straight in. "Look, I might as well tell you. I've seen you diving late at night." The disclosure was a gamble and by his reaction, she wished she had not taken the chance.

He looked away and bowed his head. A pulse throbbed in his cheek." Whatever you saw, forget it, okay? It does not concern you." His tone was stern and Naida knew better than to pursue the matter any further.

"The mist was thick tonight," she said absently, "I think I saw something strange."

"Did it scare you?" he said with alarm.

Although Naida was not about to reveal all, she felt she had to tell him about the vision or she would go mad. "Yes it gave me a fright."

"What exactly did you see?" he asked soothingly.

"It's difficult to say – an outline of a figure – the image was distorted." If anyone would understand, he would. "Do you think -could it have been Lilith?"

"Who can say," he answered vaguely.

"But what explanation can there be?" she fretted and searched his face for a clue. As if for some obscure reason he held the answer.

"There is a possibility you could have seen her." He looked serious. His breath filled the space between them.

Unwelcome sensations stirred within Naida. She longed for him to hold and comfort her. She wondered how it would feel to be cocooned safely in his strong arms. Quickly she dismissed the thought.

His eyes began to cloud over. He looked at her sternly. "I want you to promise not to go walking on the cliff late at night. Infact I forbid it for your own safety."

She suspected he may well have her welfare at heart, but he had no right to issue orders.

"Don't tell me what to do," she said sharply. "I enjoy my walks with Fenn. It's none of your business."

"Don't be so stubborn. Can't you see how irresponsible you're behaving? Fenn could bolt and go missing." He glared at her.

"Okay – I may have made a mistake staying out tonight, but I'm not stupid. I'm a grown woman and responsible for my own actions. "She held her ground defiantly.

"Well, I can't get through to you," he sighed. "I'm not wasting anymore time. It's late I have to go."

Good, she thought through clenched teeth. She was not about to stop him. Alone in the kitchen, she made herself a cup of tea and gradually her anger subsided. Half an hour later she went up to bed, feeling very isolated. Tears sprang to her eyes and rolled down her cheeks with the sheer hopelessness of it all.

Chapter 10

June ushered in with a continuation of the balmy weather. It was warming up to a heat wave. Naida sat on the slope, her paintbrush poised in mid-air with half interest. She studied the animals grazing below. Painting was therapeutic, she found, for her troubled mind. Since her talk with Howard, she had not embarked on her regular walks along the cliffs with Fenn. She just didn't have the inclination to go. Her thoughts as they invariably did, wandered to Howard. She was curious to know what was going on.

Her gaze rested on a group of sheep and cows, content, munching on the grass. It was humid. Tiny mosquitoes buzzed in the air. It struck her how the animals lived naturally in harmony. So unlike human beings with their endless striving and uncertainties – creating a tangled web. A peaceful existence was far more preferable.

A voice inside her head seemed to whisper… "It's probably not as simple as that."
She answered aloud. "Nothing ever is."

Her mind was made up there and then. She would take it upon herself to find out exactly what was going on. The possibility that Howard may be in danger played on her mind. She could not rest until she knew for certain. The best time for diving was early evening, she decided. The afternoon would be too crowded to board the boat and borrow the diving equipment.

Early evening she made an excuse to use the Land Rover and set out towards the cliffs at

Gunwalloe. The boat was deserted and unlocked. She was in luck.

Carefully she checked the diving gear, hoping it would not be missed. She then made her way to the secluded rocks where she had seen Howard dive. She took a knife with her for protection. Into the water she went, pausing to be certain all the gear was in place.

Slowly she descended, sliding head first through the murky gloom. She had not anticipated how dark it was at depth. Quickly she switched on her light, the piercing shafts cut through the darkness as she aimed downwards. She turned left, right, then back again. No sign of anything.

Gliding further along to the left – then - there it was! She slowed her pace and strained her eyes. Faintly she could make out the railing of a wooden vessel. She approached from the side. Over the years the current had pushed the vessel into a vertical position. Looking over into the ship, she could see that the decking was solid, swaying gently in a slight swell.

Once inside, she scanned her light back and forth. Her eyes widened fascinated. It was a wooden sailing ship, preserved almost intact. Obviously the cargo had been gold. The ships bell and iron stone china looked in good condition. Moving on, she found herself viewing the great windlass with its anchor chains sprawling across the deck, leading over the sides to the hawse pipes.

So this was the ship the smugglers had found. But where did Howard fit in? She had been down there long enough and seen what she wanted to see.

It was time to get back to the boat before anyone discovered the diving equipment missing.

Congratulating herself on her successful mission, Naida clambered onto the rock not a moment too soon. Two men were preparing to dive about twenty feet from where she sat, hidden by a jutting boulder. She waited until they had disappeared into the blackness below. There was no point in hanging around. To place herself in further danger would fuel Howard's insinuations of her irresponsibility.

Reaching the top of the cliff, she took one last look down, and then stopped in her tracks. Someone else stood on the rocks, ready to dive. It was unmistakably Howard. She saw him position himself ready, and then dip below the ocean surface.

The implication she had not wanted to admit, now appeared highly significant. What if Howard was involved with the smugglers? That would explain his anger and reluctance to talk when she confessed to seeing him that night. It was the last thing she wanted to believe, but there was no other explanation. "I suppose I don't really know him at all," she concluded sadly.

A whole week went by with no word from Howard. Since they had reached their, compromise, this, Naida had come to expect.

Over the evening meal Ivor remarked to Tom, "I suppose I had better deliver Howard's produce to him tomorrow, seeing he's not been round. He will need it now he's back from his fishing trip."

"There now, I expect the poor boy's busy," said Tom. He leaned towards Naida. "He been fishing last week. I been talking to the fishermen at Gunwalloe."

Naida remained silent. Whatever she suspected about Howard, she could not betray him. It was his business, she reasoned.

Then she had a thought. "Err – Ivor, I'll take the produce to him. I'm going into the village."

Ivor glanced at Tom, and then back to Naida. "Yes, sure you can," he smiled.

Naida's renewed interest in Howard obviously pleased him. "Perhaps you can deliver Mrs Dunn's produce too." He called over to Mrs Dunn. "You'll be at home in the morning, will you?"

"Oh yes Mr Tregartha – I'll be in all right," she confirmed, "I'll look forward to that."

"Of course – no problem." Naida sensed their surprise at her offer. To mask her discomfiture she adopted a blasé air.

"That's settled then, and tell Howard from us, long time no see," joked Tom.

"I haven't seen Lowenna today," remarked Naida, veering the conversation to neutral ground. "She hasn't come home for dinner."

"Seems not," replied Tom. "Treats this place like an 'otel."

Ivor shook his head. "You know what these youngsters are. She rarely eats a proper meal – just grabs a snack – then she's off again. Probably eats out with her friends."

"There's no need to worry about her going hungry," concluded Tom. "Aye, she'd soon let you know if she was."

The evening dragged despite the genial company. Naida went to bed early and attempted to sleep. Tomorrow she would see Howard again and had no idea why she had volunteered. What would she say to him? 'Howard I went diving and discovered the ship!?' Her mind whirled round and around. She closed her eyes. It was no good; her inward turmoil would not give her peace. The heat was uncomfortable. It was going to be a long night.

By morning a light rain shower had freshened the air. Naida must have slept more than she realised. Her head was clear and she felt wide awake. She began rehearsing in her mind how to tactfully approach the subject to Howard. But there was no way around it. "I'll ask him straight, was he involved with the smugglers?" It would be no use him lying, for she had seen him. She wondered how he was going to explain that. He couldn't deny they had found the sunken ship. Oh my god, she thought, he was going to be so angry if he knew she had been foolish enough to go diving herself alone.

After a quick breakfast, Naida dressed hurriedly in denim shorts and red camisole and wound her hair into a long plait. She went to collect the produce to be delivered. Packing it into the back of the Land Rover, she set off for the village.

Reaching Howard's cottage his car was not outside.

"Damn, I've missed him," she cursed. He must have made an early start. She parked the Land Rover and went up to the front door. After knocking a few times with no response, she walked round to the side window and looked in. There was no sign of life.

She turned and passed by the shed where he stored his garden equipment. The spade, fork and lawnmower were all in order. She remembered he had discussed the work involved in the garden previously with Ivor. He said he always mowed the lawn regularly to keep it healthy – never missed a week when he was at home. It was the first task he would do on his return. He took great pride in his garden. It would be unusual for him to neglect it. With a cursory glance over the garden, she noticed the grass had been left uncut.

Naida drove the short distance to Mrs Dunn's cottage. At least her journey to the village would not be in vain. Strangely on edge, she walked up to the gate. Mrs Dunn was pottering in the garden. She looked up from her weeding and greeted Naida.

"Good, I've been waiting for you. Now I can put the kettle on. I'm gasping for a cuppa. Bet you are too!"

"I'd love one," answered Naida, and then added cautiously, "Mrs Dunn?"

"Yes m' dear?"

Naida glanced at her anxiously. "Have you seen Howard?"

Mrs Dunn wiped her brow and stretched. "I'm too old for this work," she complained. "No dear, there's been no sight nor sound of 'im all week. I was going to ask you the same question. I can't understand it. If he was going on a fishing trip again, he always lets me know, so I can keep an eye on 'is place while 'es away."

101

Naida shifted the box of produce in her arms and tried to sound unconcerned. "I wonder where he's gone."

"I've no idea." Mrs Dunn shook her head. She looked puzzled. "Of course 'e could have gone deep sea fishing, he does that sometimes. That would keep 'im out all day and I don't go up there in the evenings anyway."

"I expect that's it then," Naida agreed lightly. "I shouldn't worry – he'll turn up."

She had no wish to plant doubts in Mrs Dunn's mind about Howard's disappearance and said no more on the subject. Mrs Dunn seemed reassured and busied herself making the tea. She insisted Naida try one of her homemade scones with strawberry jam and Cornish cream before she left.

On her way back, Naida's thoughts were haunted by Howard's empty cottage. Was she being irrational? I expect he has gone deep sea fishing like Mrs Dunn said. There is no reason to think otherwise, she reasoned. But - the uncut grass….?

She jammed on the brakes as she turned a sharp bend; stray sheep wandered aimlessly across the road without a care in the world. Naida cursed under her breath. Her mood was restless. It was no good; she couldn't rest until she knew where Howard was. Ivor didn't need her at the smallholding today. He had told her to take her time. Impulsively she did a three point turn and decided to make a quick detour to Gunwalloe.

The promising morning began to turn positively breezy. By the time Naida drove up to the cliffs, the wind was near gale force. She reached over to the back seat for her denim jacket, and then braved the elements. The atmospheric pressure was tangible. She glanced over the edge of the cliff. A gigantic wave was coming towards her from about a quarter of a mile away. It was so big it filled the whole area, obscuring the sky. It was awesome. She froze, mesmerised, like an unwilling participant on the big dipper. Terrifyingly beautiful. It was like the roar of concord. And then the crash, as the swell broke snowy white against the rocks. Seagulls protested overhead.

Again and again the waves struck. At last the wind dropped and the rocky bay was lit by a flood of sudden sunshine. Naida relaxed and began to descend the cliff path. A wet smacking noise came from the rocks below. From Naida's viewpoint it was difficult to tell what it was. As she got nearer a distant cry like a human baby drifted upwards, cutting through the sound of the sea.

Naida moved cautiously. Coming closer she saw a grey seal buttressed among the boulders, his whiskers silvery in the sunshine. Apparently the waves had washed him up onto the shore. On his neck was an open wound and there was a gash under one eye.

"You poor thing," soothed Naida, wondering what she could do to help. He was a handsome brute with a sleek coat. His neck hung with folds of blubber. Naida sat down on the boulder beside him and tried to comfort him. He lay slumbering on his side, giving an occasional wheeze.

Eventually he stretched and with a final hoot and a backward glance at Naida, slithered down towards the rock pool. He stopped, and then slid on plunging into his natural habitat; gliding deep, flippers rowing like oars. Naida watched him go. She had the feeling this would not be the last time she would see him.

It was late afternoon now. Naida had been so preoccupied with the seal that she hadn't noticed the time. Climbing back up the cliff path she walked for some way along the top. There was no sign or clue to Howard. She was beginning to feel hungry. It was time to abandon her search and make her way back. Tonight she would call in to Howard's cottage once more.

At dinner that evening Naida informed Ivor of Howard's absence and then she told them about the seal.

"It was pitiful, the poor thing was injured. He was such a magnificent creature. I was admiring his Roman profile."

"Yes – we get many seals down here," said Tom. "The Atlantic grey. They're bigger than the common seal."

"That's the first time I've seen one here," replied Naida.

"Seals have always been in these parts," remarked Ivor and then added, "Few men have established such a rapport with them as Howard."

"Howard?" Naida echoed with surprise. Somehow she could not connect Howard with the seals.

"Yes, didn't he tell you?" asked Ivor. "He takes great interest in them. Around breeding season he makes sure as much as is humanely possible, that they come to no harm."

"Howard has never mentioned this to me," said Naida and wondered what else she didn't know about him.

"They breed in hidden caves or on offshore rocks. Some stay around all summer," replied Ivor. "I expect Howard forgot to mention it. He can be a bit ambiguous sometimes."

Immediately after dinner Naida drove out once more to Tamarose. Driving up, the first thing she noticed was the absence of his car still. Her heart sank with disappointment. Perhaps he had gone off with the smugglers? Her imagination was running wild. There was nothing more she could do. She had no intention of searching the cliffs tonight. Her mood was despondent. The best thing was to go home and sleep on it.

Chapter 11

By morning Naida's oppressive weariness had lifted. Sunlight streamed through the half drawn curtains, lighting the room with an air of expectancy. It was going to be a brilliant day. She flung off the cover and swung her legs out of bed and marvelled at what a good nights sleep had done for her energy. She felt optimistic.

After breakfast she was impatient to get down to the beach. The thought of the injured seal with its sad face, gave her cause for concern. She wondered if it would return.

The sheltered bay beneath the cliffs was bathed in sunshine under a clear sky. The air was pure and bracing after the onslaught of yesterday's high winds. The sea gently washed the sand.

Naida breathed in deeply and looked downwards, searching the rock pools and mud slides around the beach. She fancied a wild air of excitement; of pirates and ship wrecks of a hundred years ago. Behind her, the quiet, unhurried, rustic life still went on in its secluded farms and hamlets.

She went carefully down the cliff path to reach the small curve of sand below. It was some distance from the overcrowded beach along the coastline. Tourists rarely found there way here to these hidden caves. There was no sign of the seal. Naida sat down on the rock to decide what to do next.

A cave entrance to her left caught her attention. She got up, walked over and peered inside. It was small and filled with knee deep water. Not that interesting, she thought and went out. As she stood debating where to venture next, the faint sound of a flute came distinctly from the further caves. Curious, she climbed onto a low ledge. From this angle she could see it would be easy to climb the cliff face to the next set of caves.

Stepping onto the footholds, she managed to cover a large area fairly quickly. She had just reached a part overlooking a cave entrance, when the rock beneath her feet began to crumble. Her foot slipped, sending a large boulder over the edge. It struck the rocks below with a loud crash. She steadied herself and managed to regain a safe foothold.

A hooting sound of some disturbed creature carried upwards on the breeze. With delight, Naida recognised the sound of the seal, slapping its side with its flipper. She noticed it had no gash or wounds, so it could not be the same one as yesterday.

A growl from behind a large rock made her turn. There it was the bull, next to a little barrel of blue grey fur. It was a pup. So this is what kept them ashore. The female had recently given birth but appeared in good condition.

Passages set off in all directions. Naida stood pondering which one to explore. One to the right, one to the left or the other straight ahead? Whichever one she took, she would have to crouch down and crawl into the unknown before exiting the other end.

She inspected them one at a time. As she came to the left, larger and safer passage, again she heard the flautist and followed the sound. Out the other end, she found herself in another passage, veering to the right. It was just about standing height. The end was not visible.

On she went. She seemed to be going round in a circle, until finally the space widened; then emerged into another wide cave. Water trickled down, echoing into the rock pools. A curious odour filled the air. It was as if the rock breathed.

Naida gazed into the crystal water and gasped. A shaft of sunlight shone through a crack in the cave ceiling, lighting a distorted image, mirrored in the pool. This made her turn abruptly and look up. High on the ledge she saw him lying slumped on his side, legs tied with a long chain to the rock.

"Oh my God!" Her voice bounced off the walls, her hands shot to her mouth. Alarming thoughts flashed though her mind. The smugglers must have kidnapped him – even killed him – she could hardly think straight.

"Howard!" she screamed.

He stirred, leaned up on his elbow and shot a glance over his shoulder. Naida had a mad desire to laugh with relief. He reminded her of the seal propped upon the rock.

All he said rather sleepily, was, "You took your time getting here."

She ran over and just in time and checked the urge to hug him. "Howard what happened to you?"

"Oh, it's a long story," he answered wearily, then raised an eyebrow and gave a short laugh. "It seems like you've saved my life. We're quits now."

Naida brushed his dubious humour aside. "What can I do to help? Have you any food?"

"First thing I need is a saw to get these damn chains off," he said, then added, "At least they left me some food and water and I can move, if somewhat limited."

"That was noble of them," she observed scornfully and was surprised at her protective feelings towards him. "What would have happened when the food ran out? Did they intend coming back?"

"I doubt it," he answered, "but I wasn't unduly worried. I knew someone would find me sooner or later."

Naida pursed her lips in exasperation. "I shouldn't think anyone visits these caves."

"Well you did. Mind you..." he reflected, "I did start to get concerned yesterday when the weather reached gale force."

"I should think so," she answered in dismay.

"What are you doing here anyway?" He shot the question so unexpectedly she blushed.

She didn't want to admit that she had been worried and had been searching for him. Guilt swept over her. To think she suspected him of dealing with the smugglers. She winced at the thought.

"I was exploring the caves," she answered. "Yesterday I came across a seal washed up on the beach. He's in these caves with a female and pup."

"I heard them too, when I was brought up here. It was too dark to see anything," he said, and then asked, "Do you know your way back?"

"I think so."

"Or perhaps you would like to stay here with me – just the two of us," he teased and nodded towards the chains. "I am at you mercy."

"How can you joke at a time like this?" she countered and marvelled at his resilience.

It seemed nothing could throw this indestructible man. He still looked dangerously handsome, despite the growth on his chin, his face smeared with dirt and the dishevelled hair. Or maybe that complemented his rugged attraction, she thought wryly. Taut muscles sprang firm from his short sleeved tee-shirt. His faded denims were splashed with wet seaweed. Against Naida's better judgement she would have seriously considered his suggestion.

"You want to be careful what you suggest. I could keep you here as my prisoner."

He grinned broadly, "Nothing would please me more."

Naida ignored his remark and adopted a capable tone. "Did you get a good look at your kidnappers?"

"Shall I make a statement now officer?" he drawled with thinly disguised sarcasm.

She gave a tight smile. "Well – what did they look like?"

"There were two of them. One was a big red headed guy. The other was also big with mousy brown hair and a face like a weasel. I won't forget them in a hurry," he replied.

At least it could not have been Petros, Naida thought with relief. "Right – the best thing I can do is go for help."

"Okay, but don't forget where I am," he mocked and stretched out like a lazy tiger.

"No chance," she returned. "Just stay where you are."

"I'm not about to go anywhere," he muttered dryly, jangling the chain. "A farewell kiss?" he asked.

Naida swallowed her cutting retort and turned to re-enter the passage. She took one glance back and almost weakened at the sight of his forlorn expression. She then realised he was feigning dejection and taunting her.

"Go straight to the police station," he called after her. "It will save time. Those men can be unpredictable. They may return to make sure I can't identify them."

"Yes of course," she shouted back. "I'll be as quick as I can."

She crawled back the way she had come and emerged to a surprise audience of seals, grunting at the unexpected intrusion. There was no time to stop.

Naida's appearance on entering the police station caused quite a stir. All eyes turned in her direction. She hadn't had time to think about tidying her dishevelled clothes. Her white tee-shirt was now smudged with mud, which also splattered her face and limbs. Her hair, tied with a red bandana, had dried with the sea spray into wild spiral gypsy curls. The desk sergeant eyed her up and down. She stood before him like a nomad on the defensive, green eyes sharp as a wild cat.

"Yes Miss?" he ventured cautiously. "What can I do for you?"

"Please can you help me?" she blurted out, unaware how absurd her story would sound. "A man has been kidnapped. I found him chained to a rock in a cave. Can you come quickly – and bring a saw?"

"Hang on, hang on, just a minute," replied the sergeant, looking more and more incredulous. "Let me get this straight – a man has been kidnapped you say?"

"Yes, yes, it was the smugglers," she persisted. "Hurry please. We must get him out."

The sergeant smirked and exchanged glances with his colleague. "Now look girl, you come in here with tales of smugglers and kidnappers…"

"Yes!" Her expression became more urgent.

The sergeant sighed. "Sure, and I'm King Arthur."

Naida straightened. "This is ridiculous. You think I'm mad? I tell you – There's a man down in a cave at Gunwalloe."

Two policemen sorting through some paperwork tittered in the background. Naida stood erect, pressed her lips firmly together and drew in her breath. She said in an authoritative voice. "It is your duty to investigate all complaints. If you fail to do so, I am sure you are aware of the consequences. I know my rights," she stated.

"Very well, very well," he relented, and then called wearily to a junior policeman. "George, go with the lady and report back!" He then turned to Naida. "Before you take our George 'ere on a wild

112

goose chase, I'll 'ave your name and address please."

Naida looked hard at him and muttered impatiently. "Naida Batis - Old Moorstone Farm. Okay. Can we go now?"

"Old Moorstone Farm eh? You must be the girl staying with the Tregartha's then?" recalled the sergeant. "Of course I know who you are now. I've seen you at the Fisheries Inn – didn't recognise you covered in all that grime."

Naida glanced down at her clothes. "Oh, I must look a sight. Well, now do you believe me?"

"I guess I have to," he answered stiffly. "Off you go then George? Looks like we're on to something 'ere."

The over enthusiastic young policeman practically vaulted over the desk. He rushed Naida to his car and sped off, roaring along the country lanes at full speed, sirens blaring. All the way he bombarded her with a barrage of questions. Obviously, so far, his work had not been very exciting.

Naida led him past the seals and through the passage. Howard was sitting on the ledge, calm and cool as when she had left.

"At last," he murmured lazily, "Hi George."

"Well I'll be buggered." George sat down on a rock and scratched his head. "Howard Elliot! So it's true"

Howard smiled faintly. "I suppose nobody believed Naida's story."

George gave a sheepish grin and said in defence. "You've got to admit it did seem a bit far fetched."

"Now you lot will have your work cut out solving this crime," joked Howard. "No more long tea breaks for at least a week."

"This is what I've been waiting for," enthused George, "Something to get my teeth into. If I crack this one I'll be up for a promotion."

Howard rolled his eyes derisively. "Well get your finger out and free me from these chains or we'll be here all day."

George, who had become completely overcome with events, leaped up, took the hammer and chisel and snapped the chain. Howard shook his ankles free and jumped down from the ledge. His legs buckled under him with the impact.

"Are you okay?" asked Naida.

Howard steadied himself, "Just a bit stiff."

"I bet you can't wait to have a shower. And then you should rest," said Naida taking charge.

"You'll 'ave to call in at the station first," affirmed George eagerly, "to give a statement."

"Can't that wait till tomorrow?" Naida asked with exasperation. "You can see the state he's in."

"Well. That was my orders," persisted George.

Howard took a few steps to the entrance. "Give me a break George. I'll be in a better condition tomorrow for questioning."

George was unrelenting. "It's not up to me. Orders is orders – full stop!"

"I'll tell you what –"said Howard, turning back to face the young policeman, "If I go home and freshen up this afternoon, I can call in to the station this evening. I'm sure sergeant Eames won't mind."

George scratched his head again. This habit was beginning to aggravate Naida.

"I don't know, I could be in trouble," he said, and then added reluctantly, "Alright then, but make sure you turn up."

"Don't worry George – you know where I live."

Listening to their familiar exchange of words, Naida grasped the fact that they knew each other well.

"Come on," she urged, "let's find your car Howard?"

"Let's hope it's still there," muttered George

They scrambled awkwardly through the passage. Howard greeted the daylight with an ecstatic shout.

"Freedom!" he called and raised his arms, reaching up to the sun.

Naida was looking towards the sea. Her attention had been caught by faint rhythmic flute notes.

"Listen – can you hear that?" she whispered.

"No – it must be the wind," said George and then turned to Howard, "Let's go."

Howard grinned. "I never realised how good fresh air can feel."

"Well you can spend as much time as you like in it," said George. "But right now we have to get back."

Ivor, Tom and Mrs Dunn were sitting round the kitchen table, sipping large mugs of tea waiting for news. Eager eyes turned on Naida as she entered. They all spoke at once.

"What has happened Naida?" asked Mrs Dunn.

"We hear you found Howard." said Ivor.

"Sergeant Eames phoned with the news. How is Howard? Is he alright?" asked Tom. "Something to do with the smugglers?"

"The sergeant couldn't give us any information until Howard's made a statement," said Ivor.

Naida sat down wearily. "He's fine. He was abducted. I don't know the full story; we'll have to wait until he's rested."

"There now, what did I tell you?" said Tom. "There's bin talk of smugglers. He's lucky to be alive."

"Who's lucky to be alive?" Lowenna walked in through the door.

"Howard was held prisoner by smugglers," replied Ivor. "Not to worry, he's okay now."

Lowennas face turned white. "What - Smugglers?" she stammered

"Aye – and this is our heroine." Tom patted Naida on the back.

"Oh – no," Lowennas voice cracked, and then she inhaled deeply. "Looks like I've missed all the excitement."

Chapter 12

Howard had been at the police station all evening. Naida received a phone call to report there also, as the key witness. She knew she would have to co-operate with their enquiries. She would have to tell the truth.

"What were you doing in the caves Miss?" asked Sergeant Eames.

Naida took a deep breath. "I have been walking the dog in the evenings and had seen Howard diving on a number of occasions. I suppose my curiosity got the better of me."

Sergeant Eames drummed his fingers on the desk. "I see – and what happened next?"

"I decided to dive myself to find out what was going on." Naida lowered her eyes. "I found the sunken vessel and when Howard hadn't been seen for a few days, I had a strong feeling I should explore the caves." With her hair tightly braided and wearing a long demure black crinkle cotton dress, she looked the picture of innocence. How could anyone berate her?

"That was a stupid thing to do," stormed Howard. Her virtuous appearance was obviously lost on him.

"Not a very sensible action to take Miss – no," agreed Sergeant Eames.

Howard's eyes were hard as steel. "Those men could have spotted you and I dread to think of the consequences."

Sergeant Eames continued, "As I understand it then, it was you Howard that they spotted – then what?"

"Blake and I had discovered the ship," he answered grimly, "He's gone away till the end of the month. I knew someone had been looting the gold and it was just a matter of catching them."

"Why didn't you inform us?" asked Sergeant Eames in a stern voice.

"You know as well as I do Sergeant," explained Howard. "I had absolutely no proof."

"And you were determined to get it eh?" Sergeant Eames spread his hands flatly on the desk top and scrutinized Howard.

"Too true," Howard went on intently. "Do you know who that vessel belonged to?"

"No – but I'm sure you're going to tell me." Sergeant Eames adjusted his jacket.

Howard squared his shoulders. "My great, great uncle – Henry Elliot."

"So you found the log book then?"

Howard nodded. "It was in the strong box."

"Almost the last piece of the jigsaw," replied Sergeant Eames, checking over his statement. This case was getting interesting, he thought. As a boy he had dreams of being an airline pilot, but had to forgo this after being catapulted off his skateboard by the local bully and landed in a bucket down a well. The village bobby had hauled him out. After his stay in hospital left him with a limp and fear of heights that put paid to that ambition. As an angry young man he drifted into a career in the police force with a mission to bring all bullies to justice.

Over the years not much had happened in this sleepy village and he had become complacent in his boring routine. In the 60s they had hired a radio and wiled away the days listening to the Beatles and Engle Bert Humperdink. When Elvis died they had a wake and drunk so much cider they had to close the station for the day.

"Not quite," Howard cut in quickly. "We have yet to catch the looters."

"Descriptions?" ordered the Sergeant.

Naida watched Howard's face darken with displeasure. He went on to describe the men. "Big fellows they were too. That fateful night I dived down to the ship as usual and caught them removing the gold bars."

"And that was when they saw you," stated Sergeant Eames.

"I was so incensed," continued Howard, his anger sharpening. "That I swam straight for them."

Sergeant Eames stopped, pen poised. "That was foolhardy."

"I know that now," admitted Howard, and then went on, eyes blazing. "They came at me with knives. I made for the surface, but it was too late."

Naida pictured the scenario and shuddered. She tried not to think what the consequences could have been.

Howard shook his head. "There wasn't much I could do – with a knife at my throat and another prodded in my back."

Sergeant Eames leant over the statement on his desk. "Right," he said bluntly, satisfied. "We should have this cleared up in no time. They're opportunists, we call them looters!" he shrugged disdainfully.

"I'm convinced they're the same men who were smuggling in drugs last year," said Howard, as the thought crossed his mind.

Naida recalled the rumours at the Fisheries Inn.

Sergeant Eames put down his pen and leant his elbows on the desk. "This time we're going to nab 'em good and proper. Will you help us pull 'em in Howard?"

"It'll be my pleasure," Howard replied with determination. "What do you want me to do?"

The sergeant stretched up and pointed a finger at Howard with authority. "Get your divers down at Gunwalloe tomorrow night – I'll get my men well hidden nearby."

"No problem," agreed Howard. "I want to put these criminals where they belong."

Sergeant Eames face cracked slightly with a lop sided grin. "Good man. You can go now" he concluded, then glanced towards Naida. "You too Miss and keep well clear of those cliffs."

Naida stepped out into the night with Howard. He walked her to the land rover. She stopped and looked up into the star-studded sky, avoiding his eyes. The silence was broken by the sound of the sea, gushing onto the shore in the distance. Magic was in the air.

Adrenalin pumped through Naida's veins, caused by the excitement of the day. Howard's mood matched hers. On impulse he drew her close and hugged her in a friendly embrace.

"I feel elated," he whispered, brushing his face against her hair.

For a moment she leant against his chest, feeling safe and secure. His body was strong and comforting. She wanted to lose herself in his fresh aroma.

"I hope they catch them," she said quietly'

"With all the information we've given them?" he tilted her chin and captured her eyes. "They're sure to."

Naida prayed fervently that they would, otherwise she would have to disclose Petros involvement. She shivered and drew away from him.

"I had better be getting back – it's late," she murmured.

He caught her hands in his. "The night's young – can I take you for a meal," he suggested. "I want to thank you properly."

She was tempted. It would be a perfect ending to the evening. Inwardly she sighed and gritted her teeth. She would have to be strong.

"Not tonight Howard – I really am tired," she insisted and opened the car door.

He smiled acidly. "I am not one to begrudge you your beauty sleep. Goodnight I'll see you when this is all over."

She nodded silently and drove off.

Naida was ready for an early night. She switched off the table lamp. However, her mind was still active with the events of the day. She lay awake, over tired and unable to sleep. Later into the night she heard a continuous thudding coming from the top of the house. Eventually she realised it was someone pacing back and forth. It could only be one person…

Naida decided to investigate. She grabbed her robe and quietly stole up the hall. As she reached the staircase the pacing grew louder. . She stood outside Marianne's door and listened. She called her name softly, so as not to alarm her with her presence and waited. The pacing stopped. There was no movement, just silence.

Naida tried again. "Marianne – It's me Naida. Can I come in?"

She heard the bolt lifted. The door opened a crack. Two frightened eyes stared out.

Naida smiled with concern. "I heard you walking about. I can't sleep either."

The door creaked wider. "Are you alone?" Marianne shot an anxious glance over Naida's shoulder.

Naida stepped aside. "Of course I am. Everyone's asleep."

Marianne put a finger to her lips. "Shh!" she hissed and beckoned Naida inside.

Naida's eyes widened in amazement at the beautiful embroidered cushions and quilt on the bed. A large medieval tapestry in a wooden frame stood against the wall, half finished.

"Why – it's beautiful!" she exclaimed.

Marianne hid her face in her hands. "It's for the church."

Naida looked surprised. "The local church – I didn't know you - ?" She stopped unsure.

Marianne didn't answer. She began to tremble.

122

Naida observed her quizzically. Something didn't add up. "It helps to talk about things sometimes," she coaxed gently.

"It's a secret."

"I won't tell a soul – I promise."

Marianne eyed Naida with suspicion, her arms wrapped tightly around herself. "I just want to go to sleep."

Naida tried desperately to read Marianne's expression. All she could see was fear. "If you tell me what's troubling you, it may help you to sleep. I'm on your side."

Their eyes locked together. Naida waited for a reply. Marianne averted her eyes. She then glanced back furtively and opened her mouth as if to speak. But no, her attention was drawn to the tapestry.

"Why can't you sleep?" Naida broke the silence.

Marianne seemed tormented by her secret thoughts. She hesitated, and then turned sharply towards Naida. "It was a night such as this – I couldn't sleep," she began falteringly. "I – I took Fenn for a walk."

The wild look in her eyes made Naida clutch the arm of the chair. "Go on," she whispered.

Marianne took a long shuddering breath. "I walked over the fields – into the wood. I saw a glimmer of light coming from the old disused church." Her eyes glazed over. "I can't remember." Naida waited. Marianne turned away again. It was no good; she was enclosed in her private world. Naida surveyed the room. The tapestry held her attention. It looked so beautiful; she walked over to admire it. As she drew closer she gasped. From

123

across the room the jewel colours had captivated her. Now she could see it in detail.

"It's the devil and his right hand man, Mestopholes." Her head jerked back to Marianne, cowering in the corner. "What's going on?" she demanded.

Marianne stumbled across the room and collapsed in a crumpled heap onto the bed.

Naida hurried over to her. "Are you alright?"

"Go now," shrieked Marianne. "Go – I'm tired now." She lay back breathing heavily.

Naida was shocked. She'd had enough drama for one day and wondered what else she was about to discover. "Can I help – can I get you anything?"

Marianne, her breathing back to normal, looked coldly at Naida. "No- get out."

Alarmed, Naida took a step backwards. The change in Marianne's character shocked her. She sought for words to pacify her, but knew at that precise moment it was useless. Quietly, she moved across the room and shut the door behind her as she left.

Naida tossed and turned on her pillow, her mind refusing to sleep. It was the early hours before she eventually drifted off. The state of her subconscious caused erratic nightmares. Petros jeering face whirled around in her head. Howard, laying face down in the water tormented her dreams. She had to escape. She couldn't take any more. She found herself drifting to the window and out into the muggy air. Over the fields, entering the dense wood, she went. The darkness was oppressive, until she finally came out to a clearing. In front of her loomed the ancient disused church. She floated closer and peered through a crack in the door. Black candles glowed on the altar. Hooded figures were dragging something up the aisle. Naida strained her eyes to see. A great blanket of fear enveloped her. The sound of the flute came so loud, it cancelled out her dream.

Chapter 13

What did he say?" Lowenna interrupted.

Ivor, talking on the telephone, motioned for her to be quiet. "Fine – yes, thank you for letting us know Sergeant Eames – and you'll be in touch." He replaced the receiver.

"Well, what's the news?" demanded Lowenna.

Naida heard the raised voices as she headed for the kitchen.

"It's turned out," began Ivor, "A loud commotion was coming from the Fisheries Inn. Two men, the worse for drink, were boasting about their haul of looted gold – a fight broke out with some local lads – the police were called and the men have been arrested."

"But that's great news." Naida's face lit up. "That means Howard won't have to go after them tonight."

"Howard's at the police station identifying them now." Ivor gave a wry smile. "It sounds like they may be the ones that abducted him."

Naida expelled her breath with relief. "How long will Howard be at the station?"

"I don't know, these things take some time," explained Ivor. "Once the men are charged it shouldn't be too difficult to track down any accomplices they might have."

Lowenna looked agitated. "Hmm," she muttered. "I'm going out for a while."

No-one commented. They were all too preoccupied with the unexpected turn of events.

The telephone rang at precisely four o'clock. Naida, who was the only one in at the time, picked it up.

"Naida?" The voice she was waiting to hear came soft and low across the line.

"Howard," she breathed shakily. "How's it going?"

"I'm still at the police station," he answered wearily. "It's all over now. I'm leaving for home shortly. The two men have been charged. I recognised them immediately. I told you I would never forget their faces."

"Oh, I'm so pleased Howard," she sighed. It was a great weight off her mind. "I'll let the others know."

"I have to go now, someone's waiting to use the phone. Tell Ivor I'll call round this evening."

Before she had time to reply the phone went dead. "Howard?" Instinctively she spoke into the mouthpiece. She stared at it in stunned silence and then walked over to the window.

Spots of rain tapped lightly against the glass. The sun was still shining. A rainbow arched across the sky from the outbuildings, in a kaleidoscope of colours and disappeared behind the far trees. Naida blinked furiously. For some reason she wanted to cry. Whether or not with relief she didn't know.

Howard arrived at seven thirty, extremely unruffled. After what he had endured, any lesser soul would have wilted by now, reasoned Naida. Unlike herself, who had such an unsettled night, he positively glowed. However, a refreshing shower had banished any trace of her tears that had spilled without warning, mirroring the rain on the window.

Howard sat on a chair nearest the door, in dynamic form.

Lowenna arrived back, her face fixed in a glazed smile. The earlier doleful expression had vanished.

"Howard – how are you?" she enthused, cancelling out all other questions being fired at him.

"It's all been sorted out Lowenna," he answered.

Lowenna glanced sharply at Naida, and then turned consolingly back to Howard. "I'm so relieved for you," she declared. "Those men deserve to be thrown in jail – and I hope they throw away the key."

"They'll get what's coming to them," stated Howard calmly.

"Good," snapped Lowenna. "Have the police taken all the gold from the cliffs at Gunwalloe yet?"

Howard shot her a questioning look. "How do you know it's there?" he demanded. "No one has been told the location yet. The police want to keep it quiet until they've made a thorough search."

Lowennas face turned pink. Her eyes narrowed. "It's obvious – that's all," she stammered. "I mean, that would be the first place anyone looting gold would hide it."

Howard nodded. "Good guess Lowenna," he observed.

Lowenna smiled sweetly. "It's wonderful to have you home again Howard. When will it be safe to go scuba diving again?" she drawled.

Ivor turned to his daughter. "Give the boy a chance!"

Naida began to feel dizzy. She had the sudden urge to leave the room. Lowenna's shrill voice grated on, monopolising the conversation.

"I won't have time for diving," answered Howard. "The seals are beginning to congregate and pups being born. I'll be busy keeping an eye on them – steering them to a safe cove."

This rekindled Naida's interest. She was intrigued at this surprising side to Howard's character.

"Do you look after them every year?" she asked.

Howard sat back in his chair and ran his fingers through his hair. "Yes," he said shortly. "This year I hope to make a bid for an area of the beach."

"What- buy it?" asked Lowenna in amazement. She clearly thought the idea absurd.

Howard nodded. "There's a cove at Gunwalloe ideal from the seals point of view. The landing is easy – plenty of rock pools and the pups cannot be pushed by the tide and washed away to drown."

"That will cost a fortune." Lowenna pulled a wry face. "What a waste, just for seals."

Naida was appalled by the younger girl's insensitivity. She said nothing. But she caught Howard's compassionate eyes and held them. He had no need to justify himself.

He addressed Naida when he answered. "The reward for discovering my ancestor's vessel and leading to the looters arrest will enable me to purchase it."

"That's wonderful," marvelled Naida, her face lit in admiration.

Howard was surprised at this rapport with Naida. Her keen response was unexpected. "It will mean the seals can breed without human interference and I can deal efficiently with any injuries."

"I congratulate you," said Ivor wholeheartedly exuberant with the outcome. Naida noted that he looked extremely proud. "At least son, some good has come out of this harrowing experience."

Lowenna was beginning to look bored. Nursing sick and lactating seals was obviously the last thing she intended getting involved in. She expelled an impatient sigh and turned her attention to Mrs Dunn.

"How long will dinner be?" she enquired. "I'm famished."

Mrs Dunn, bent double over the oven to retrieve the warm plates, straightened. "I'm dishing it out now my girl."

Throughout the meal, Lowenna took little part in the conversation. She concentrated on eating ravenously, and then promptly left the table, informing everyone that she wanted an early night.

Naida had half listened to Howard all evening, as he held centre stage recalling his story. Her thoughts were elsewhere. Marianne's tapestry kept returning to haunt her. She needed some answers. But who could she trust? She wanted to understand what was happening here. After dinner she excused herself and departed to her room.

The following week passed quickly. There was plenty of work at the smallholding to keep Naida occupied. By the weekend she was looking forward to going to the beach for a swim. She assumed Howard must be organising his seal sanctuary at Gunwalloe and was tempted to take a trip there herself to see how the injured seal was faring. It was as good a place as any to go swimming.

Naida tied a turquoise sarong over her bikini, grabbed her towel and went.

The main beach at Gunwalloe was crowded. Before going in search of the seals, she immersed herself in the cool water. She swam out, and then floated, allowing the waves to drift her gently back to the beach. Refreshed, she then strolled slowly along the waters edge towards the caves. Part of the way she had to clamber over some rocks until she came to the cliff path.

At the top, the sea breeze was invigorating. She stood transfixed, attuned to nature's vast display, the sun dappled foam rising and falling. At any moment, she imagined a procession of playful dolphins would dance on the waves in time to the high notes of the wind.

Further along she could make out the cave where Howard had been held prisoner, and swallowed. This was the first time she was returning to the spot overlooking the sunken ship. She turned back towards the tightly packed white washed cottages, spilling down the hillside. Her attention was caught by a single magpie nearby. How did the saying go? "One for sorrow…" An involuntary shudder made her turn away sharply. She hurried on.

A sheltered bay came into view and the unmistakable sound of the seals could be heard. Howard was resting on the sand between two rocks with his back to the cliff face. Without him noticing, Naida climbed carefully down the cliff path. She crept up behind him and put her hands lightly over his eyes.

"Guess who?" she said with mischievous impulse.

Howard's strong hand came over hers and pulled her around to face him. "I would know that sing song voice anywhere," he teased, "What brings you here?"

She was about to say she was just passing. But on reflection it sounded absurd. "It's a good day for a swim," she explained airily. "And I wanted to see if my seal was still here."

"Your seal?" He raised a quizzical eyebrow and fixed her with an amused expression.

Intuition told her that he was pleased with her unexpected visit. He was in top form.

"You know what I mean," she answered. "The one I came across last week."

"Yes the seals from the cave." He pointed to the rock pool. "They're over there."

The bull slept with one eye open, basking in the warmth of the sun. He looked contented. Just a mark was left on his head where the gash had been.

Naida sat down beside Howard and took in the tranquil scene. "I'm amazed – this is such a peaceful haven."

Howard picked up a pebble and let it fall carelessly through his fingers. "Many stay until they have recovered from there injuries, without being hassled." He spoke with dedicated conviction. "The pups can learn to swim in inland pools instead of the rough sea."

As if to prove this, two cubs began flapping about, churning the water into mud. Naida watched them attempt to move their hind flippers and raise their heads calling to each other.

"They're singing," explained Howard. "After dark their hooting sound carries on the breeze. The ancestors called it the ancient song of the seals."

"How beautiful." Naida shut her eyes and lifted her face tranquilly to the sun. "This is important to you isn't it?"

Howard plucked another pebble from the beach and tossed it into the water. "The sea and its inhabitants should be important to us all."

"I agree." Naida opened her eyes and let her gaze cast a net over the ocean "The force of the sea is an underlying energy of life. Wave motion gave life its original direction. All children were taught this on the island of Cyprus. It's built into every one of our cells. "

"It demands respect." Howard paused on this thought, and then continued. "With one breath the elemental rulers of the waters could destroy us, if gathered together in wrath."

Naida nodded fervently. "We must learn to use it properly and not pollute it."

Howard turned to her with empathy. She looked as vulnerable as the baby seals. "All things are but one and there is no part of us that is not of the Gods."

How well he understood. "We are all linked inextricably together," she affirmed. A pleasant sensation, caused by the uncanny realization that she had known Howard far longer than this short season, came over her. They seemed tied together from a limitless past.

He leaned across and gave her a friendly hug. "We all have our part to play – however small."

Her body trembled at his firm touch, her large eyes wide and serious, gazed into his.

He observed her smooth velvet skin and sensitive mouth. "I bet you're a Pisces," he spoke softly. "As delicate as a coral shell - complex as the changing tides." He bent his head and found her lips inviting.

She surrendered as she knew she would, accepting his kiss with quickening breath. It was sweet and light. Slowly they drew apart.

"How did you guess?" she murmured, the strong vibrations still connecting them.

"You couldn't be anything else really – could you?" He raised an inquiring eyebrow. "I recognise your affinity with water and it explains why you're always trying to swim in the opposite direction."

"What do you mean?" she shot back indignantly.

"You have that mystical quality, with one foot in two worlds." His penetrating gaze bore into her with a hypnotic effect, deep as the turbulent sea.

She was aware that the powerful forces of nature could be something to be reckoned with and tore her eyes away. "It's not true," she responded.

"Are you so sure?" he replied. "We are both of the mutable water element. I'm a Scorpio. You're like me Naida – a free spirit."

It was true. Her mind had been opened to so many new sensations since coming to this place. Before, she had been suppressed – the dutiful daughter, behaving as was expected of her. She needed more than convention could offer.

"We appreciate the power of nature," he continued. "The earth, air, fire and water. We are not meant for city life. We need space."

He was right about her, she thought with irritation. Whenever they were alone together his presence became overpowering and somehow dangerous. She must have been mad to entertain the idea of coming here today. To allow herself to be stung by a scorpion would be a mistake. Her legs felt surprisingly weak as she stood up.

"I –I have to get back now," she stammered.

"Its early" He glanced up at her, nonplussed.

She bit her bottom lip and looked away.

"You've only just got here," he sighed. "Don't go cold on me now."

She turned as if she hadn't heard him and carried on up the cliff path.

"Why do you have to go?" he shouted.

"I can't stay," she yelled back, adamant in her mind that to give in would be disastrous.

He followed her to the top of the cliff. They faced each other, his eyes blazing.

"What is it with you?" he stormed. "You came down here to see me and don't say it was just to see the seals. I can feel it in your kiss, for God's sake. You don't know what you are doing to me Naida."

"You don't understand do you?" she shrieked.

No, I don't. Put me straight."

She had to be firm. There was no other choice. "I told you, I don't want to get serious – I don't need this."

"You could have fooled me!" He squared up to her mightily provoked. "At least I've kept my distance. I haven't come looking for you, however hard it's been. I'm not the one who has been seeking you out!"

"What?" she snapped.

He folded his tanned, muscular arms across his chest. "Come on, it's written all over your face – you find it hard to resist me," he taunted her, goading a response. "I was just about to grant your wish and ask you to an intimate lunch together, before you so childishly ran off."

This pushed her over the edge. "You – how dare you," she spluttered. "I wouldn't go out with you if you were the last man on earth." With that she flung herself into the land rover and in her haste promptly stalled it. She cursed. The next attempt ignited the engine and she drove off at high speed.

"You must accept the truth – you cannot swim against the tide, Naida." The futile words he shouted after her were lost in the wind.

Who did he think he was? How dare he imply…?" Her thoughts screamed over and over again in her head. That's it! I want nothing more to do with him. It's over - finished! That's if it ever started, she mused wryly. The man was no more than an arrogant, chauvinistic pig – and why she had ever thought herself attracted to him was laughable.

By the time she arrived at Old Moorstone Farm, she had cooled down. His outburst had affected her like a slap in the face. He had also made her realise how unaware she had been of her own foolish behaviour towards him. She had no intention of a repeat performance.

Tom was sitting out the front as she drew up. "You're back early – thought you'd be at the beach all day."

"I had a swim and then decided I'd had enough," she said abruptly. She was in no mood to explain.

"Oh – I see," said Tom, taken aback at her tone, "Are you okay girl?"

Naida softened. "I'm alright – just a bit of a headache coming on." She had not meant to be short with Tom. She smiled. "It's so hot. I think I've had too much sun."

He tilted his hat and gave her a discerning look. "It's easy to get dehydrated in this heat. Drink plenty of water."

"I will." She went quickly inside, wanting to be alone to gather her thoughts.

She poured herself a glass of mineral water and took it to her room, feeling slightly guilty. Her head was not aching. Despite being exasperated with Howard, a new found strength had surfaced. It filled her with determination to fight any notions of infatuation she harboured towards him. If this emotion could be bottled, she considered, it would be in great demand. Tonight would be the start of a new episode. Life was too short to be serious.

Early evening she emerged from the shower, almost believing she was a new person. Her present state of mind had mentally washed away all the negative emotions of the past. She dropped the towel and straightened her body in front of the mirror. At this stage in her life she was perfectly formed with satin smooth skin, firm and shapely.

She said aloud. "I am a new person in control of my life." This evening she would grace the Fisheries Inn with her presence and try out her lighter personality. Instead of just grabbing whatever clothes came to hand, she was selective, inspired to make an effort.

Her red palazzo pants and matching cropped top, she felt was ideal for her new image. They made a statement – bold and carefree. Flat red pumps completed her outfit with a young and casual undertone. Her hair, caught up in a scrunchie cascaded in a mass of cork screw curls, complemented by the silver hoop earrings.

Her entrance at the Fisheries Inn was head turning. A number of boisterous youngsters were crowded at the bar. Soon the place would be filled with new faces – tourists and day trippers. Ivor ordered drinks for Naida and Tom whilst they found a table.

As the evening progressed, various friends of the Tregartha's joined them. The atmosphere was convivial. Naida was feeling confident and glad she had come. It was a great diversion. A young guy amongst the group at the bar had been staring quite openly at her all evening.

Naida offered to buy the next round of drinks. Boldly she squeezed through the throng to be served and found herself next to her admirer.

"Stand back – give the lady room," he said loudly to his friends, and then winked at Naida. "You better watch this lot!"

Naida laughed. He was tall and gangly with an open likeable face, topped with a mop of shoulder length blonde hair – probably younger than her, she observed. However, they were fun and lively – just the tonic she needed.

"Are you locals?" she asked, brashly making conversation whilst waiting to be served.

"Originally yes. Most of us have been away at university," he grinned. "Can I get you a drink? I'm Mark by the way."

"I'm with friends," she smiled. "Thanks anyway."

He leaned back against the bar and eyed her shrewdly. "You're not with your boyfriend are you?"

"No," she said, and then with more force. "No-I'm not."

"Then stay and have a drink with us," he shouted in her ear above the din. "No ties or commitments eh? You're my kind of girl."

She was tempted. By the time she had been served he had talked her round to accepting. She delivered Ivor and Tom's drinks to their table, and then returned to the bar for the remainder of the evening.

At closing time, a radiant Naida rejoined Tom and Ivor. She hadn't enjoyed herself so much for a long time. Mark was obviously smitten with her.

"It's my mates twenty first next Saturday – will you come?"

"Yes – I'd love to," she answered without hesitation."

He loped backwards towards the door, smiling. "I'll meet you here at eight thirty. Okay?"

She waved, feeling incredibly light headed. Things had turned out well tonight. "See you then," she replied.

Chapter 14

The following morning Tom teased her about the impression she had made on the young man.

"He was fair taken with you alright," winked Tom."

She took a sip of her tea. "He was just being friendly."

"Nay he asked you to a party. He must o' bin keen," Tom assured her. "Someone's twenty first?"

"Yes, that's right," replied Naida, wishing Tom wouldn't harp on about it. She looked at her plate and attempted to change the subject. "Mrs Dunn never breaks the yolks when frying the eggs. I wish I knew her secret."

"Easy really love. Watch me next time." Mrs Dunn came over with the kettle to top up the teapot. "It's probably young Mathew Haynes. His mother told me a few weeks back he be coming of age."

Naida took a bite of her toast. What a drag! She realised with grim resignation there was no chance of them dropping the subject.

"They don't live far from Howard – he knows them well," went on Mrs Dunn, and then nodded across at Naida. "Go and enjoy yourself dear."

Naida stiffened. The mention of Howard's name unsettled her. Her resolution to forget him was going to be aggravated if her new found social life overlapped his.

The heat wave continued all week. It was too hot for work. Naida helped out when needed, but like the others, she spent a lot of time sitting in the cool of the kitchen or outside under the overhanging tree.

141

She could see Marianne's window from here. She noticed it was shut and was concerned that the room must be stuffy in this heat. With all the events of late, she had not been so observant and vowed to eventually get to the crux of Marianne's problem.

With determination, thoughts of Howard were pushed to the back of her mind. She refused to let herself feel hurt. As long as he kept away she could cope. She intended to enjoy this party.

As she squeezed into her black Lycra cat suit, she felt excited and confident it showed her curves to full advantage. Her long hair hung loose and pretty around her shoulders. Medium heels completed the outfit. The effect was sexy – almost an act of defiance.

All the same, on her way to meet Mark she began to feel apprehensive. He stood waiting patiently outside the Fisheries Inn. Disappointment clouded her earlier optimism. She fought desperately to rekindle it.

His gaze widened as she stepped out of the land rover. "Wow!" he exclaimed, his eyes rolling.

She began to lighten. "You approve?" she smiled, and then took in his appearance and laughed. "You're crazy!"

He was wearing a garish pair of multi coloured Bermuda shorts, a tee shirt with a rude motif and yellow Reeboks.

"Hey – you only get one shot at this life and anyway it's too hot. I'm a cool dude right?!"

"Okay, I believe you," she quipped, and then added with humour, "I don't know if I want to be seen walking in with you – it won't do my image any good!"

"Don't worry – all my mates dress like this," he assured her.

True to his word, the others were clad in similar attire. The girls however had made more of an effort, outdoing each other in the shortest dresses or brief satin shorts. The party was already in full swing.

The house was not far from the sea, reached by a narrow lane which ran parallel to Howard's cottage. French windows were open wide and people spilled out onto the lawn in high spirits. Delicious aromas wafted from the barbecue. Mark grabbed hold of Naida's hand and pulled her towards it.

Although the food was appetizing, Naida did not feel hungry. Mark obviously was ravenous, the way he devoured whatever he was offered. Naida stuck to one glass of white wine all evening, not even attempting to sample the punch. Mark introduced her proudly to his friends and their host Matthew. Later they joined in the dancing on the lawn, before drifting back inside.

The room was crowded. Naida looked about her, watching the dancing. She caught sight of Matthew with a small group. He gave her a friendly wink, and then turned his attention back to the man beside him, who was half hidden by another group of people. Naida heard the man say. "Never be fooled by a woman, they are fickle and changeable." There was no disguising that voice, thought Naida. God, its Howard!

"That's a bit primitive," answered Matthew.

"They are primitive," Howard replied.

Naida had no wish to eavesdrop any longer and pulled Mark over to dance. As he whirled her around to the music, she was sure Howard had been referring to her. She glanced in his direction and noticed Lowenna hanging on his arm. They both saw her and Howard nodded curtly, whilst Lowenna gave a sly smile.

Naida felt her cheeks burn. She had no idea they would be here tonight. Lowenna had certainly kept quiet about it. However, she shouldn't be so surprised, after all the girl regarded Naida with indifference, bordering on silent contempt.

The remainder of the evening they spent on opposite sides of the room. Naida kept catching Howard looking at her, but every time she caught his eye, he looked away. Mark stuck to her like glue, trying to impress her with his jokes. He wasn't too bad at impersonations either. She played along – bubbly, full of life – the centre of attention. Kicking off her shoes, she began dancing barefoot – wild and wanton.

Inside she felt a fraud, a puppet on a string. Howard's presence had thwarted her plans to forget him and sent her emotions haywire. Being so near and knowing she couldn't touch him was too much to bear. She loved him and she hated him for having this power over her.

The thought of him made her weak. His rugged good looks, his eyes, his sensuous smile… It was only physical attraction, she told herself. It had nothing to do with love. He was impossible. She realised that however much she partied and convinced herself she was happy, it was superficial. It would not console her. She stayed until midnight, and then made an excuse to Mark and left.

The hot June weather suddenly turned wet. The atmospheric pressure began to depress Naida. Work was her only distraction. Fortunately business was booming. Ivor was unable to leave the smallholding and Naida had taken over all the deliveries. Up until now Howard had come to collect his own produce or Ivor had taken it to Tamarose.

"I won't have time today," Ivor told her over their lunch break. "You don't mind delivering Howard's produce, do you?"

She couldn't think of a suitable excuse, after all it was her job. Anyway, she would have to face Howard sometime and learn to live with his presence around the village.

The rain splashed relentlessly against the windscreen as Howard's cottage came into view. Naida took a deep breath. She was sure she could handle the situation now. In her mind she planned to be friendly but aloof and leave as quickly as she could.

She parked the land rover and cut the engine. Almost immediately Howard appeared. He must have been waiting. Naida's heart began to pound rapidly as she opened the back door of the car and lifted out the box.

Howard hurried over. "Here- let me…" He reached out. For a split second, briefly their fingers touched. Naida took a sharp intake of breath as a spark passed between them. He placed the box aside and turned to her. Their eyes locked, drawn like magnets. Naida began to tremble. She couldn't help it. The sexual tension was electrifying.

"Naida," he whispered, his hand brushing a stray curl from her face. "I'm sorry."

She tried to speak. The words stuck in her throat.

"All those things I said to you on the beach," he continued, a slow smile curving his mouth. "Please forgive this ignorant fool."

All her caution was lost in his penetrating gaze. "Yes," she managed weakly – sensible intentions forgotten.

Both were sensitive to each others reactions. The intense passion between them was at boiling point. Slowly he bent his head closer and gently claimed her mouth. With soft feathery kisses, he savoured the sweet taste of rain on her lips. He took her hand and began kissing the tips of her fingers. Lifting her hair, he kissed her neck, her ears, and her closed eyelids. Her insides melted.

Acknowledging her response, he returned to her mouth, this time with more urgency. Her arms wound around his neck as if she had no control over them. He parted their lips just far enough to whisper huskily. "Have you ever made love in the rain?"

"No," she breathed, oblivious to her rain soaked voile dress, displaying her curves and taut nipples.

He kissed the rain from her face, running his fingers through her long hair. "I always fancied you with wet hair," he murmured hotly against her cheek. "You're shivering – I don't want you to catch cold," and with that he lifted her into his arms and carried her into the cottage.

Naida had the sensation of being in a pleasant dream. In a feverish state he worked the buttons on her dress. The idea of resistance toyed briefly with her thoughts, but was soon squashed as she allowed her dress to fall lightly to the floor. The hypnotic power in his eyes turned him into an irresistible love controller.

She delighted in his pleasure as he removed her wispy underwear, as if she was a gift wrapped especially for him. He feasted his gaze on her naked loveliness.

"You're beautiful," he breathed.

As she impatiently unfastened the belt of his trousers, his lips found the velvet smoothness of her neck. He lifted his head and gasped as she quivered eagerly at the touch of his erection. His fingers moved down to stroke the rounded slopes of her breasts, like ripe peaches.

Cupping gently, he kneaded the soft texture of her flesh, exploring every inch. He caressed her arms, her back, her tiny waist, arousing with firm, smooth strokes and light fingertip movements. Naida's skin came alive, her senses on fire. As he reached her thighs she mouthed a weak protest.

"Please," she moaned. A sharp sensation deep in the pit of her stomach took her breath away.

They read each others thoughts, accepting and taking it in turn to be pleasured.

"Oh yes Howard," she gasped, unashamedly excited and she found herself responding urgently.

"You're my sweetheart," he cried, laying her down gently on the hearth rug. Their bodies moist and fragrant from the soft rainfall, entwined, igniting each other. Thrill after thrill swept through her body with magical harmonising rhythm. The rest of the world disappeared.

"My beloved," he cried as their passion soared to a climax.

"Oh my God," shouted Naida as waves of pleasure overtook her and surged again and again through her body.

Outside the rain splashed against the walls and pounded on the roof, as if to wash away the past. Their passion spent, they lay content in each others arms.

"Watching you dance at the party was driving me insane – I love you Naida," Howard said in a low voice. He smiled down at her. "Promise you won't go cold on me again – okay?"

Her long eyelashes flickered up at him. "I promise," she whispered.

He ran a finger down her cheek, thoughtful. "Why Naida – why did you run from me that day at the sea? I thought we were getting on so well."

She gave a deep shuddering sigh. "Things happen sometimes – events catch up with you. I was afraid."

He leaned up on one elbow and stared at her. "What do you mean? I don't understand."

She stared back at him – wide eyed. "I do love you Howard. But - but if anything should happen – just remember I do and try to understand."

He looked baffled. "Understand what? And what could possibly happen?"

She knew she was being evasive. But her background had been so different to his and the traditions of her people would be anathema to him. He didn't deserve to be compromised.

Her lips trembled. "Please don't – don't ask me any more questions. Let's forget about everything except us – you and I together at this moment."

Not wanting to spoil the magic he sighed and held her close. "Alright, we'll say no more about it. Darling Naida my beautiful mystery woman."

Sudden sunshine threw spectrums of light streaming through the window. The rain had ceased and evaporated in the heat like dried up tears.

Chapter 15

"I want to marry you and I won't take no for an answer," stated Howard after much soul searching, unable to contemplate life without her.

Naida folded her arms and leant back in her chair. "What sort of proposal is that?" she exclaimed.

"What more do you want?" he replied, forthright as ever. "You don't expect me to go down on one knee, do you?"

She faked an indignant expression. "Why not? Anyway this is all rather sudden."

"A simple yes would do," he said as if it was reasonable advice.

"Everything has happened so quickly." She was being deliberately evasive. As the weeks went by the more difficult it became to tell him and the Tregartha's the truth. "I need time to think."

"What's there to think about? You and I are meant for each other and you know it my love." He leant across and kissed her. "Okay, I'll give you till the end of the month – then I'll expect your answer."

They were sitting in the farmhouse kitchen. Howard had just dropped in to see her, as he frequently did these days, before going fishing.

"I'll see you this evening," he said as he got up to leave. "I'll take you to the Roseland Peninsula – land of the roses." He kissed her once more, just as Lowenna came through the door. Sullenly, she went to the fridge, and then plonked herself down at the table.

Howard tilted his head to one side. "Hi Lowenna," he said brightly and when she ignored him he went out whistling to himself.

After he had gone, Lowenna turned sharply to Naida and said through gritted teeth. "You two seem to be seeing a lot of each other lately."

Naida leant her elbows on the table. "Yes Lowenna – we do," she answered flatly.

"Well, well what a turn up – I never thought Howard was open for manipulation," Lowenna replied with unconcealed sarcasm.

Something snapped inside Naida. She had just as much as she could take from the girl. Eyes blazing, she said. "Look – it has nothing to do with you whatsoever. Howard and I are very happy together – we may even have a future together, so you had better get used to the idea and if I were you I would stop acting like a spoilt child and grow up."

Lowenna's jaw dropped, stunned. Naida rose from the table. Immediately Lowenna seemed to change her tune.

"Now wait a minute Naida, perhaps I have been a little bit unkind and – err – unfriendly towards you," she said slowly, choosing her words carefully. "I didn't mean to," She put on a little girl voice and innocent face. "Let me make it up to you – I'm going to be in the village most of the day. Meet me there later – let's say three o'clock and I'll treat you to a cream tea, please Naida?"

Naida hesitated. She sat back down again and drummed her fingers on the table with impatience.

A quick glance across at Lowenna confirmed the girl's remorse. Naida's anger subsided. She ought to give the girl a chance to make amends she thought soberly.

"Alright – but don't ever, and I repeat, ever cause trouble again."

Having cleared the air Naida felt a sense of relief. Lowenna had needed someone to give her some straight talking to. Hopefully she would now see the error of her ways. Naida could appreciate that it must be hard for her. After all the girl had all the attention before she came on the scene and it would be preferable to be friends.

It was five to three when Naida jumped into the land rover and headed for the village to meet Lowenna. The sun was just beginning to cut through the clouds. The valley stretched below her. On the hillside a few scattered cottages overlooked a church and beyond the grassy banks sloped down to the sea.

Parking the land rover at the edge of the village, Naida made her way to the tea shop. She had gone no more than a few yards, when a screech of brakes stopped her in her tracks. Petros wound down the window. "Get in the car Naida. I have come to take you back home."

Naida froze. Eventually she found her voice. "I've told you Petros, I will never go back. How could you expect me to?"

Petros glared through the open window and adopted a menacing tone. "If you won't come willingly I shall have to report back to Father, and we will both return to take you by force."

"How can you be so cruel?" Naida grabbed onto the window and pleaded. "Don't do this to me."

His face grew dark. "You're time is up – I'm bored with this place."

Her spirit returned. She retorted angrily. "Bored are you? Is it getting too hot for you Petros? I know about your involvement with the looters."

His black eyes glared at her with contempt. "You have found out too much for your own good. You and that boyfriend of yours are becoming a problem to me – poking your nose in where it's not wanted."

She backed away from the car and stood her ground. "You are the one who is trouble Petros, you always have been. I will keep quiet only if you leave me alone."

"Huh! You're bluffing, you wouldn't dare tell anyone – anyway you haven't a shred of evidence. You can prove nothing," he said arrogantly. "I can see these people you are staying with must be important to you."

"Yes they are," she snapped. "They've given me work. I can now support myself. I don't need you or anyone."

"Really?" Something in his tone changed. A sly expression crossed his face. "If I decide not to tell Father – and I'm not saying I won't. What will be in it for me?"

She knew immediately how his mind worked and asked carefully. "What do you mean?"

His eyes narrowed. "I'll do a deal with you. It won't hurt me, I suppose, to hang around a while longer – and if it's to my advantage… And there are other entertaining diversions," he smirked and she

153

wondered what he meant. He leaned towards her. "You could be of some use to me. We might as well get as much out of these yokels as we can."

Naida resisted the urge to slap him with great difficulty. "If you do anything to upset these people Petros, I'll – I'll…"

"You'll what Naida – kill me?" he said dryly.

She clenched her fists at her side. "Yes – yes, I'll kill you. God help me I will." Steely determination showed in her eyes.

He laughed derisively. "As long as you do as I say, they will remain ignorant of the fact that you are on the run."

He watched her reaction. She stood rigid, her mind racing. Would she ever escape the Batis family? They held her in their clutches, using her for their own ends.

"You cannot force me to go back. I'm over twenty one. I can go where I please."

"Ah, but that is not how our Father sees it. You are his property – you know how it is."

She did know how it was. Andreas was a law unto himself. Proud – one who held fast to the old traditions – a dangerous combination.

"Obviously I have no choice." She lifted her chin and looked him straight in the eyes. "What is it you wish me to do?"

"Now you're being sensible." He relaxed back in his seat. "For a start – your silence, which goes without saying? Secondly, I want half of your wages."

"But that's blackmail!" Nothing surprised her about him anymore.

154

He shrugged. "Call it what you like – I call it good business logic. That's the deal or..." he gave an impatient sigh. "You will hand it over every week here at this spot. If these people think so much of you, it should be easy to get a wage rise."

She felt defeated. There was nothing she could do but resign herself to his demands. At least she would play for time. This would stall him for the present. She had no illusions that he would keep to his word.

"Alright - but I warn you – if you come anywhere near the farm..." she stopped.

"Agreed." He began to wind up the window. "Meet you here same time next week." He gave a salute and with an evil laugh, drove off.

Naida stared after him. She wasn't so much shaken as furious. She knew she could well afford to live on half her wages. Ivor had been more than generous. But to be obligated to Petros made her seethe.

"How dare he!" she said aloud. The thought made her shake with rage. What could she do but play along with him for now? A couple passing by looked at her with alarm. This shook her back into reality. Gathering her composure, she went in search of Lowenna, who must be wondering where she was by now.

A bell chimed as Naida opened the door to the tea shop. Glancing around, she noted that most of the little tables adorned with pretty red checked cloths, were occupied. There was no sign of Lowenna. Naida went up to the waitress and asked if she knew Lowenna and if so, had she been in?

"I know who you mean," replied the waitress. "No dear, I've not seen her today, sorry"

Naida looked at her watch. Half an hour had passed since she'd had her heated discussion with Petros. As she walked back to the land rover, there was so much on her mind; she wasn't unduly worried about missing the cream tea. Nevertheless, she did wonder what could have happened to Lowenna.

By seven thirty Naida had showered and changed into her Levis, teamed with a nautical navy and white striped sweat shirt. She tied her hair back, securing it with a red chiffon scarf, and then pulled tendrils down to soften the effect. She observed herself critically in the mirror. Despite the recent rain, she still had a good tan. There was no need for make up, just moisturiser and a quick dab of red lip gloss.

Howard drove up ten minutes early. He was in the kitchen talking to Tom when Naida came in. After a hard days work he still looked alert. He rose from the chair like a panther and greeted her with a kiss on both cheeks.

"All set? We'll go to St. Maws, okay? I want to show you the harbour. We can have a bite to eat at the Inn."

"Sounds good," she enthused. Looking at him clad in denim jeans and jacket, her insides stirred. It was as if she was beginning to touch the edge of happiness. It was so fragile and she suspected with her situation it could be fleeting.

There was something special and tranquil about driving through the countryside, Naida decided, as they travelled along the winding lanes shaded by leafy green trees, leading unexpectedly past a scattering of cottages set beside quiet waters. Deep water creeks penetrated miles inland. A maze of beautiful wooded inlets met to form the great estuary of the Carrick roads.

Reaching St. Mawes, Naida noticed it had an almost continental appearance.

"It's beautiful," she sighed and realised that he had put a lot of thought into this evening.

Leaving the car, Howard led her down to the small harbour. A mass of colour from the sails of many tiny yachts and dinghies darted across the water. Howard took her hand, turned it over and kissed her palm.

His eyes searched her face. "Have you ever experienced anything like this, Naida?"

"Not quite." She averted her eyes, unsure whether he was talking about the view or not.

He glanced out over the ocean. "This is a beautiful place – yes, a place to bring a beautiful woman." He turned back to face her with a gleam in his eyes. "Doesn't it invoke you to fall in love?"

"I have fallen in love with Cornwall and…" she stopped and shuddered, remembering her meeting with Petros this afternoon and what he and his family were capable of.

"And…?" he insisted.

She knew he wouldn't rest until she had said it. "And you," she finished softly and melted into his arms as he pulled her close.

Lost in each other, within the remoteness of the entrancing semi-circular bay, they stole tender kisses. In the freedom of the wind the seagulls sensed their delight, in the supreme precision of their flight, riding the up draught with hardly a flap of their wings.

The bracing sea air sprayed lightly against their faces as Howard and Naida made their way from the harbour a few paces across the coastal road to the square, abundant with roses. To reach the entrance of the Inn they climbed a flight of steep steps from the narrow street. Howard ushered them to a window table overlooking the creek. They could see the boats at anchor and to their right, green, pine covered hills. It exuded charm and character, thought Naida.

Howard must have read her thoughts. "I knew you would like it here," he said, "enchanting, isn't it?"

"Yes," she agreed. There was nowhere she would rather be at this moment.

He sighed. "I could sit here for hours. Just look at that view across the rooftops down to the harbour and estuary." He shook his head in awe. "It's romantic, don't you think?"

It was just perfect, thought Naida. If only life could be perfect. She knew that was unrealistic, but hey, she could dream! That far away look was in her eyes when she answered. "Yes it is."

Howard turned back to face her. "Sweetheart, I hope you are giving some thought to my proposal." He paused at her worried expression. "But I won't rush you. I shouldn't have mentioned it so soon. I'm sorry. You must know how impatient I am."

Naida didn't answer. Her eyes misted over.

"Not another word – I promise. Now lets enjoy the evening," he finished and turned his attention to the menu.

Naida nestled contentedly into Howard's shoulder as they drove home through the dark narrow lanes. The meal had been superb. Drowsy and relaxed from the wine, she put her trust in Howard completely, knowing he knew the area like the palm of his hand. This was just as well as they sped steadily through the pitch black night.

She stirred, her eyes half open and murmured her thoughts aloud. "I wish we could drive on forever, over that hill into eternity."

He smiled in the darkness and squeezed her hand. "You are funny. What a strange mind."

In companionable silence they drove on, until they pulled up in front of the farmhouse.

"It's a shame the evening has to end." His voice was low and husky, as he held her close, not wanting to let her go.

The moonlight lit their features, their lips met hungrily. The kiss was long and searching, somersaulting Naida up to her silver star, flying over, around and down to earth again. It was time to say goodnight. She let herself in quietly and prepared for bed.

Although the wine had made her sleepy, thoughts of the evening and Howard kept her awake before she finally drifted off to sleep, only to dream of him. He was waiting at the altar and turned to watch her gliding up the aisle. He looked so handsome as he turned and smiled at her. They became Psyche and Eros from Greek mythology. Psyche, dressed in her bridal gown, hair decked with flowers, holding a bunch of white lilies. Eros stood behind her, armed with bow and golden arrows. His face was hidden from her.

Around them water nymphs danced in celebration of the marriage. Eros handed Psyche a letter. As she opened it she looked into his eyes for the first time and saw they are filled horror.

Psyche, now seated on the rock was staring pensively out to sea. In her hands she holds the bedraggled remains of her bridal bouquet.

Naida awoke abruptly from her nightmare feeling uneasy. Had she screamed out?

No one else seemed to be awake. Getting out of bed, she went over to the window and looked out over the fields, eerie and still in the moonlight.

Her eyes wandered back into the room, resting on Lilith's poetry book. Drawn towards it as if in a trance, she picked it up and the page fell open. "When I glimpse you in your house of glass," she paused. It was the same poem as before. Was Lilith trying to communicate? Maybe she was urging her to sort things out before it was too late? Naida shivered and got back into bed.

The following morning Lowenna was already at the breakfast table when Naida walked in."

"What happened to you yesterday afternoon Naida?" she asked. "I waited ages for you in the tea shop."

Naida sat down and gave her a dubious look. "That's funny – the waitress said you hadn't been in."

160

"Which waitress was that?" asked Lowenna, spreading her toast thickly with honey.

Naida poured herself a cup of tea and proceeded to give Lowenna a detailed description of the waitress.

"Oh her," replied Lowenna, about to take a bite of her toast. "She wasn't there when I arrived. They work in shifts you know."

"Not to worry," Naida shrugged. It was hardly of major importance to her now. "No harm done, we can go another time."

Lowenna smiled condescendingly, her eyes wide as saucers. "Of course we can, but not today. I'm going surfing. I want to make the most of it while the weather's suitable."

Naida returned the smile and sipped her tea. "Yes, I would if I were you. Anyway Howard takes up a lot of my time."

"Does he?" Lowenna bit deep into her toast.

Naida wondered if she caught a hint of irritation in Lowennas voice. No – she was getting paranoid. The girl deserved a chance.

Chapter 16

The letter arrived with the morning post the following morning. It was waiting on the mat when Howard returned from fishing. It looked, by all accounts, an ordinary sort of letter. Except he noticed later, when he retrieved it from the bin for inspection, it had no stamp on it.

This mornings work had been successful and he was feeling pleased with himself. This afternoon he had arranged to take Naida to St. Ives. She had shown him some of her sketches and he was most impressed.

"You have talent Naida. The artist colony at St. Ives should interest you," he had said and smiled as he recalled her enthusiasm.

He stooped to pick up the post, flicking through the pile of letters. The bills he threw onto the table. Ah, he mused, a letter from Amsterdam from Hans. It was always nice to receive news from old friends who had shared his fishing trips.

Then he came to the white envelope with his name printed in large capitals. He opened it absentmindedly and looked at the words, then looked again. No, it couldn't be – someone must be playing a practical joke. Whoever it was had a warped sense of humour.

After his initial reaction of shock, he dismissed it as nonsense, screwed the letter up and threw it in the bin. He made himself a light lunch, showered and then went out to meet Naida.

The weather was glorious. The day couldn't have been better for their trip to St. Ives. Howard sang along light heartedly to the music on the car radio. With buoyant anticipation he drove up to the farmhouse.

Naida saw him from the window and ran outside to meet him. The sun enhanced her cascading hair, rippling with burnished lights. Howard's admiration was evident as he took in her radiant face and slim tanned body, clad in white shorts and halter neck top. They greeted each other and set off.

Howard parked the car just above the traffic free town of St. Ives. Despite the invasion of holidaymakers, the old fishing quarter around the harbour had survived remarkably. Naida found it a bustling town thronging with visitors.

They strolled past a complex of stone cottages lining the cobbled lanes and alleys, bedecked with masses of geraniums and other summer flowers, growing from window boxes and hanging baskets. Fish cellars and shops jostled with art galleries and studios.

Naida took Howard's arm and pulled him into one art gallery after another. She was thrilled to discover so much local art.

"How picturesque," she commented on the beauty of the bright paint lighting up the old grey stone of the artists' studios in sail lofts and quaint cafes.

"The artists who live here guard its beauty most zealously." Howard informed her as they continued through the confusing maze of narrow streets with odd sounding names.

Naida stopped by a street sign and attempted unsuccessfully to pronounce the name. "It's fascinating. I bet it's steeped in legend."

"There is a legendary saint," said Howard. "St. Ia who founded the town – came over from Ireland in the middle of the fifth century. Legend says she sailed over on a leaf."

"What a lovely story," mused Naida, and then added on impulse, "I must buy a picture of St. Ives to take back to London. I would like a souvenir by a local artist."

"I see," Howard replied curtly.

Puzzled by his tone, she turned to face him.

"It's up to you," he said coolly as they stepped into yet another gallery. He pointed to an attractive oil painting of St. Ives harbour.

Naida's eye was caught by the title, Gunwalloe Church Cove. "Look Howard, I must have this one." The little church in the rock was just visible above sparkling violet water at sunset.

Howard gave an impatient sigh. He looked serious. "Does this mean you have made your decision to return to London?"

"What – what do you mean?" she said absently, still intently observing the painting. "Just look at those colours. The brush strokes are superb – such freedom of hand."

Howard's forehead creased into a frown. "This painting is to be a souvenir of your short stay in Cornwall – is it not?"

She shot him a disconcerted glance. "No – I didn't mean…"

"You didn't mean what?" he stressed.

Naida sensed he was displeased and couldn't understand why he was so upset.

"You just said yourself," he continued. "The painting is to be taken back with you."

"I suppose I did. No – I didn't - I mean – oh I don't know why I said that," she stammered, her thoughts confused.

"Well, are you returning to London?" he demanded.

Why did he have to spoil things? "I haven't come to a decision yet Howard. Don't rush me. You know our agreement."

He was not about to let the subject drop, his tone was quiet with suppressed anger. "It sounds to me you know exactly what your plans are."

"That's not true, stop putting words into my mouth." Tears of frustration welled up behind her eyes. If only she could give him the answer he wanted.

"You are mistaken Howard. I was so carried away with this place – I just spoke without thinking."

"Ah yes sweetheart, often that is when one tells the truth," he replied with irony.

"Don't be ridiculous. You can be so stubborn. Let's not spoil the day." She tried to diffuse the situation and added," "I'm going to buy this painting now – okay?"

Howard didn't answer. He remained where he stood, distant and frosty.

Naida went to find an assistant, who then wrapped the painting whilst providing a lengthy story about the artist and history of the cove.

When Naida turned round Howard had gone. She searched the gallery but there was no sign of him. Surely he wouldn't abandon her here? She quelled the rush of panic. It was possible to take the bus back, but to part on such a sour note was more than she could bear. How foolish of her to be so tactless. Tucking the painting into her bag, she sat down miserably on the bench in the centre of the gallery.

She didn't notice the man in dark glasses who sat down behind her until he spoke.

"Hi Chiquita, how goes it?" The sly voice was instantly recognisable.

Naida spun round. "Petros!" She gasped.

He slowly removed his glasses and smirked. "I see you are alone. Where has your handsome escort gone, eh?"

"What on earth are you doing here? How…" she began. "My friend will be back in a minute."

His black eyes narrowed. "I doubt it. I've been watching you and he's got the hump with you for some reason."

Naida glanced around furtively. He made her feel like a criminal. "He will be back I tell you." She tried to sound convincing.

"Don't worry, I'm going. I'm not here to pester you. It was coincidence I happened to bump into you today, dear sister," he stressed with sarcasm. "So I thought I might as well say hello. After all one shouldn't ignore one's family, should one?"

"Well, you've said it," she snapped coldly. "Now go."

"I have a more interesting assignment anyway." He arose, replaced his sunglasses and glanced down his nose at her strained face. "Just one thing Naida, don't forget our meeting as arranged." He turned away from her and sauntered out of the door.

Naida's mood plummeted, the day was ruined. How could Howard leave her like that? Blindly she ran to the door and reached for the handle. Before she managed to open it, the door swung wide, nearly knocking her off her feet.

"Oh!" She cried.

"Sorry – are you alright?" It was Howard. He held her arms, steadying her.

The angry retort she was about to make stuck in her throat. She lowered her eyes. "I think so. I wasn't looking where I was going."

The incident appeared to have broken his irrational mood. He laughed derisively. "That seems to be a habit of yours Naida."

"Where have you been?" she shot back, suddenly aware of the hollow emptiness she had been left with.

"To get this…" With nimble fingers like a magician, he produced a small package from behind his back and handed it to her. "To apologise for being so pig headed and impatient"

She laughed and the colour came back to her cheeks. "You didn't have to do that Howard. Now you make me feel guilty."

"Don't!" he chided and with a single smooth movement ushered her outside. "I think it's time for a coffee."

They made their way to the nearest café. Naida was thankful to fate for giving her another chance. They would start the day afresh.

"Open it," coaxed Howard as they sat waiting for their coffee to arrive.

Naida untied the string and revealed an exquisite sculpture of a mermaid, delicately hand painted with great care by a local artist. "Howard!" she exclaimed. "It's beautiful."

His blue eyes glowed with warmth when he looked at her. "She reminds me of you – that illusive quality. See how she gazes into the distance as if she sees beyond the veil of earthly existence."

Naida felt almost unworthy. "I shall treasure her forever."

The waitress interrupted their conversation with the coffee and Naida carefully put the statue away.

"How about hiring a rowing boat and taking a trip around Seal Island," suggested Howard, suddenly not wanting to waste a minute.

"Good idea." Naida finished her coffee. "Great – I'm ready."

They left the café and headed for the attractive harbour. Dotted with a variety of small boats, it was the main focal point. Naida impressed Howard by insisting on doing her fair share of the rowing.

"You've done this before," he challenged her as she pulled on the oars with expertise.

She gave a confident smile, delighted to be his equal on common ground. "I'm used to messing about in boats. As a child I spent long summers in Cyprus by the sea."

Looking back, those summers had been idyllic, when her Mother was alive. Naida had no complaints about her childhood. Andreas was a stern disciplinarian and could be cruel, if he was allowed. But her Mother more than compensated for any of his shortcomings with her fierce, protective love for her daughter. Naida remembered Petros as a brat, but nothing she couldn't handle.

"I'm always learning something new about you – such hidden talent," teased Howard. "You never cease to amaze me."

Naida stopped rowing and let the oars drift. "I guess I was lucky to enjoy such wonderful family holidays. I took it for granted at the time."

Howard dropped his hand over the side and let his fingers slip through the water. "I should like to meet this family of yours."

She hesitated, and then said. "They go away a lot since Mother died."

"Your Father?" he inquired, wondering who she meant by "they…"

She stiffened and concentrated on rowing again. "My step- father actually – he travels a lot."

"How often do you get to see him then?"

"Occasionally –look, why all these questions?"

He gave her an odd look. "Such mystery, this family of yours."

"Not at all," she returned, attempting to sound casual. "There's no hurry to meet them, is there?"

"It's just that you never talk about them." He leaned back reflectively with his hands behind his head.

"Okay, it's no big secret. I don't get on with my step-father and brother, that's all. And I still find it hard to talk about my Mother." Her lips trembled. A lump came to her throat. The last thing she wanted was to dissolve into tears in front of him. She took a deep breath and waited for her emotions to subside.

He looked sympathetic and said gently. "I understand how you feel Naida – I've been there too."

"I know," she murmured and took another deep breath.

He sat up and straightened his arms at his side for support. "This won't do. We are supposed to be enjoying ourselves. Move over." He took the oars from her and with determination swiftly guided the boat around the island until a secluded beach came into view. "This looks a good place to swim."

Naida jumped out onto the hot golden beach as Howard grounded the boat. She removed her sandals and felt the soft sand trickle between her toes as she walked. The sensation was soothing. Turning around she saw Howard hopping on one foot, whilst attempting to remove his trainers. She laughed. He ran up to her, grabbing her playfully around the waist.

"What do you find so highly amusing?" he scolded.

She laughed again, lost her balance and fell against his strong hard chest. His arms dropped away and he sprang back.

He then held out his arms and smiled. "Come here."

Slowly she moved towards him. He reached out and gave her a big bear hug. She remained in his comforting embrace with her head on his shoulder. All her worries and grief disappeared. He had this healing effect on her.

"You make me feel so good," she murmured.

"And I am so lucky to have found you," he replied silkily. "Now - how about that swim."

The cool water was invigorating as they swam close to the cove. Although they were both strong swimmers, Howard thought it wise not to venture out too far. Naida floated languidly, allowing the waves to glide her gently back to the shore.

Howard swam out a little further to where the rocks ended. The sun promised to shine at least for the rest of the day. Tucked away from the busy harbour, Naida imagined herself shipwrecked alone with Howard on a desert island.

She was smiling secretly at her fanciful thoughts, when the sound of a speedboat approaching interrupted the tranquillity. The roar grew louder as it came closer. Too close, thought Naida. She stood up in the shallows with a start as Howard shouted.

"You fool; you missed me by an inch!"

The boat sped off, scanning the water into circular ripples. Naida caught a glimpse of the occupants and her jaw dropped. It looked remarkably like Petros with a blonde. The girl glanced back over her shoulder and Naida could have sworn it was Lowenna. No – it couldn't be? She must be mistaken. Petros and Lowenna? It was too mind boggling.

She turned to Howard and shouted. "Are you alright?"

He was swimming back towards her. "Yes, but another inch and that boat would have sliced me in two."

"You could have been killed." She embraced him as he reached her.

"Did you see who was in the boat? I didn't get a good look at them. The force of the water sent me flying." He looked back over the now calm water.

She bit her lip. "No, it happened too quickly." Then she noticed the blood on his shin. "Look – you've cut yourself." She untied the scarf from her hair and made him a makeshift bandage.

"I must have banged it against the rocks." He started back up the beach and she followed. "If I get my hands on that irresponsible idiot…!"

Naida seethed inwardly, sure it was Petros. He would have some explaining to do this time. She couldn't let this go on. She must tell Howard the truth. Lying back on the towel, she planned how to go about telling him. He leaned over and kissed her. Her heart melted. Where I begin, she wondered.

"I could stay here forever, but I think it's time to go," he breathed softly.

The moment for confession was gone, Naida concluded miserably. "I suppose so." She opened her eyes, squinting in the sun. "How's your leg?"

He reached down and removed the blood soaked scarf. "That's certainly done the trick. It's not bleeding any more."

"Thank goodness for that." Naida leaned over to examine the graze. "It's not too deep a cut. You ought to get a proper bandage on it though."

He stood up and stretched. "I think I'll live," he said making light of it. "I've endured worse you know."

"Maybe, but it's not pleasant." Naida ran her fingers through the length of her hair and shook the sand out.

He raised an eyebrow and smiled down at her. "I can see I'm safe in your hands."

"It's no joke Howard," she shot back with an anger that surprised her. "You shouldn't have gone near those rocks." It wasn't him she was annoyed with; it was the owner of the boat and herself. Everything had gone too far. How on earth had she allowed Petros to blackmail her? One thing had escalated into another. With force she crammed her towel into her bag and stalked off towards the rowing boat.

He grabbed his things and caught up with her. "Slow down Naida. What are you getting so het up about? I'm still in one piece." He was trying to placate her. "Don't look so worried. What's your problem?"

"Nothing – nothing at all," she answered with an edge of sarcasm.

"I should think not," he reproached her light heartedly. "With your good looks and talent – and you've got me."

She began to mellow. "True," she joked, led by his light mood.

Later, she fell silent beside him as they drove back through the lanes. Low trees bowed their heads, almost touching from either side of the road, creating shadows across the ground. Sun glittered like diamonds between the leaves. Deep in thought, Naida was oblivious to it all. She couldn't bear the pretence. Her situation was becoming impossible.

Chapter 17

Howard watched the crystal waves lap against the rocks from his window. A week had passed since the first letter had dropped through his letter box. At first he had ignored them, and then they merely irritated him. But this morning he decided enough was enough. Whoever was sending him such poisoned mail must be stopped.

The first one to arrive was printed in red ink – DO NOT TRUST NAIDA. YOU HAVE BEEN WARNED. Since then the messages had become increasingly malicious. Today's letter was in the same large print – NAIDA IS A BITCH - ALREADY ENGAGED TO BE MARRIED - USING YOU. He told himself it could not possibly be true. But who…? He could stand it no longer. The culprit would have to be caught. The letters always arrived when he was out fishing. He would give it until the end of the week, and then lay in wait.

The sea spray crashed harshly against the granite stone in the distance. To Howard, in pensive mood, it seemed to be mocking him. Why was Naida so reluctant to accept his proposal? Today he had invited her to have lunch with him at Tamarose. She was due to arrive any minute. He opened the fridge door, just about to prepare a salad.

"Hi," Naida walked in through the back door and kissed him on the cheek. "I'm starving. I've been working hard all morning."

He placed the tomatoes and lettuce on the table. "No rest for the wicked!" he teased with fake sympathy.

"Huh!" She punched him playfully in the ribs. "I'll have you know I've been boxing up fruit and vegetables since eight o'clock this morning, and I've just delivered a box to Mrs Dunn."

He raised his hands in mock surrender. "Okay, I believe you. How about giving me a hand with this?"

She snatched the knife from him impatiently. "I'll chop the salad – you lay the table on the patio."

"Good idea." He retrieved an ice cold bottle of sparkling wine from the fridge: selected two glasses from the side and proceeded out into the garden. He sat down lazily and unscrewed the cork.

Naida appeared presently with the plates of mouth watering avocado prawn salad and two long granary rolls. Howard poured the wine.

Naida lifted her glass to his. "Here's to us today having a great summer."

"To us," he repeated, but it sounded more like a question.

She surveyed his closed face. "Yes to the future."

"I hope we have a future together." Only his slight questioning tone gave away what he was thinking. "I would like to think so."

She sipped her wine wondering what was coming next. He was not about to start pressuring her again, was he? She glanced away. The swish of the sea absorbed their thoughts.

Eventually he said. "You are a very beautiful woman Naida. Many men must pursue you." He studied her with an analytic glint. "How many proposals have you had, I wonder?"

"What is this – confession time?" she asked a little perplexed.

He played with the stem of his glass, spiralling clockwise. "No I was just thinking I know so little about you – about your past."

She swallowed and gave a quick laugh. "There really is nothing exciting to tell. I had one serious boyfriend – he did propose, but it didn't work out. It was a mistake. It's history." She waved her arm in a dismissive gesture.

The thought of Adam Brent, whom she thought she had been in love with, made her flinch. She had lived to despise him for accepting her stepfather's money in favour of marrying her. Andreas would not agree to her becoming an Englishman's wife and had successfully warned him off. Or paid him off, she thought bitterly.

Howard appeared to take this rationally, but his eyes betrayed him. "And you haven't seen him since?"

Although his voice sounded placid, Naida detected he was keeping it controlled?

She looked at him sharply. "No Howard I haven't. What are you implying?"

"I am implying nothing," he mused casually, elbows on table, fingers cupped together. "I just find it hard to believe that you haven't hoards of admirers."

"Howard – really, you're too much." She shook her head; her hair fell across her face.

His expression still gave nothing away. "Well," he said with a dramatic undertone. "You could be a fugitive, running away from something."

She pushed her heavy hair back from her forehead and mocked his suggestion. "Oh sure, I'm Madonna in disguise!"

He wasn't thrown. Intrigued by his own extravagant theories, he continued. "I wonder who you really are. Let me guess - an Egyptian princess seeing how the other half live. Or you could be a Russian ballerina defecting to the west?"

"Oh yes – and you could be the Prince of Wales," she quipped.

"Ah," He observed her poise faltered under his scrutiny. "But I know who I am. The question is - do you know who you are?"

She raised an eyebrow. "I should hope so." His mesmerizing gaze was confusing her. She mustered her inner strength and rose to the challenge. "Anyway, you can talk; you're a very complex man. The night we met at the barbecue you appeared, without reservation, to have me summed up already. I found you overbearingly chauvinistic."

"Okay – so I was wrong about you," he admitted. "I am obviously not a very good judge of women."

"Obviously!" she retorted.

He took a sip of wine, eyeing her steadily. "But who are you?"

I'm just Naida," she answered, wondering if she really did know at all. "I've come here searching for myself."

He leant back in his chair. "Yes, you are a mystery my love." He took her answer as part of the psychological game they were playing.

"For that matter," she cut in. "How many women have you proposed to?"

"None," he shot back immediately, and then added. "Only one – you."

She wasn't going to let him get away with this. "You must have had some girlfriends in the past."

"Sure – a few," he answered unperturbed.

"How serious?" She wondered why she was doggedly pursuing this line of questioning. It wasn't that she really wanted to know…"

"Drop it," he ordered.

Then she knew why! He thought it was acceptable for him to question her… but when it came to him, he had double standards. In reality he'd had many girlfriends, but had never been in love before he'd met Naida.

However, it wasn't in her nature to be churlish. At least he wasn't one of those egotistical men who loved to boast of their conquests.

"What a strange mood you're in Howard." She decided to try another tactic and manoeuvred her hand across the table into his. Never before had she thought of initiating their love making. What was he doing to her? All this talk was turning her on. The touch of his fingers, the sensuous look in his eyes, the heat of the moment – the sun. She wanted him -

now! She uncrossed, and then crossed her legs and let one stiletto dangle invitingly.

"Early afternoon?" he said in surprise, catching her thoughts.

Her breath quickened. She ran her tongue over her lips and stood up. "It's hot," she gasped and with one movement removed her cotton sundress and flung it onto the chair.

He smiled astonished pleasure. "It's a good job this patio is secluded."

She walked around the table and let him feast his eyes upon her. "It's no different than if I was wearing a bikini."

"If you say so," he replied, catching his breath; unconvinced at the sight of her tiny black lace thong and matching half cup bra.

She could see her actions were exciting him. "Want to see more?" she teased.

This side to her was new to him. He was supposed to be the seducer. But he was enjoying this. "Take them off!" he urged, attempting control.

She smiled seductively and undid her bra, revealing her soft rounded breasts; and then slipped out of her thong.

He pushed back his chair and patted his knee. "Come here," he said.

Slowly she walked around him, naked except for her red heels and stood behind him. Gently she began to massage his scalp. He leaned back and let her take over, enjoying the sensation. Reaching up, he grabbed her hand and pulled her round to face him. She perched herself onto his aroused lap, thoroughly relishing the balance of power swinging in her favour.

"Temptress," he murmured. "Do with me as you will."

Eagerly her fingers undid the buttons of his polo shirt. Gently, she lifted it over his hard chest and darted her tongue along his ear.

"You have a beautiful body – so sexy." His voice quivered with emotion.

She wriggled, her buttocks rubbing against his shorts.

"Oh – oh – easy," he muttered and quickly twisted out of them.

She dipped her fingers into his wine glass and started to lick off the sparkling liquid.

Erotically, he took her hand to his mouth and savoured each finger separately. "Delicious," he breathed against her palm, and then reached over to the glass and immersed his own fingers.

Lightly he traced a liquid path across her skin. Travelling down her slender neck, over and between the curves of her breasts, leading down to her navel, following the line, his tongue tasted the sweetness. He sucked, delicately biting her nipples. Erect nerve endings sent powerful messages of arousal to her brain. He continued down to her navel, stabbing seductively with his tongue. When he could reach no further, his fingers took over and slid with expertise between her legs.

"Oh yes – yes." She arched her back against him, spread her thighs and gripped the chair.

He looked down at the pulsating swell beneath his fingers as he manipulated her rapidly then slowly, causing her to beg satisfaction. The delay, he knew, would drive her to frenzy. She attempted to arise to allow him to enter her.

"No – not here – later," he whispered huskily. Then, not to disappoint her, he began swift strokes with his fingertips until she shuddered out of control.

Fulfilled, she lay back against him and sighed. His hands circled her breasts and began the urgent squeezing. She was soon aware he wanted more.

A smile curved her lips as she picked up his wine glass, turned to face him and poured what was left onto his chest. It trickled down over the spiral pubic hair and onto his lap. She bent her head and returned the pleasure, moving down his body with her tongue. He stretched back in his chair, content to let her lead.

She found him throbbing and knelt down in front of him. The maleness of him rose and fell as she wound her fingers around.

"Slow down," he urged.

She took her hand away and began stroking his thighs; and then returned to stroke him lightly from the root to the tip of his erection, causing him to become harder.

"Like this?" she asked. Wanting to please him she moved her hand and found her own rhythm to suit him.

He was groaning guttural sounds, his head flung back in ecstasy. "Go on – go on – you've got it now."

The thought that they may be caught at any moment added to her excitement. Kneeling before him, her lips moved to lick away the last of the wine. She probed and moulded him until he also erupted into a long howl. The force of his masculine release took her by surprise. As the spasms subsided, she sprang back, her eyes wide.

He smiled. "You're gorgeous. Come here"

Like a kitten, she crept back onto his lap. She planted a kiss onto his forehead, and then fell quiet, secure in his arms.

He stirred and looked at her. "If we stay like this all day I won't be able to keep my hands off you." He caressed her stomach, and then glanced over at the uneaten rolls on the table. "I thought you were hungry?"

"I was – but my hunger for you was more urgent. However…" she sighed, the aroma of the bread tempting her. "We will enjoy eating now." She lifted his roll and put it to his mouth, and then reached for her own.

The heat of the mid-day sun and their frantic love making left them perspiring with a honeyed glow. Like lazy caterpillars they sat entwined, languid and loose, unwilling to end their pleasure. Softly they continued to caress each other, until Howard felt the tide rise in him again. Lifting her up, he stood up.

His lips curved into a smile. "See what you do to me – you shameless sex Goddess. We can't go on like this – someone is sure to catch us."

Swiftly he took her into the cottage and laid her gently down on the sofa. "I won't be long, stay there." He disappeared, leaving her in anticipation.

She let her mind drift leisurely onto another planet. In celebration of their love they danced around the galaxy and pirouetted towards Venus. She never wanted to come down to earth again. The aromatic fragrance wafting from the bathroom added to her intoxication. What was he doing? She closed her eyes with contentment.

The next thing she knew, his soft lips were brushing against hers and she was being lifted up and transported to the bathroom. Gently he lowered her onto a velvety cloud of bubbles. She lay back and let him sponge every part of her body with gentle gliding strokes.

"Wait a minute," he breathed huskily and left her to relax in the creamy lather. He then returned with a single glass of pink champagne. She opened her eyes to see him climbing into the bath to face her. He smiled and tilted the glass to her lips, and then to his own; sharing replenishment – sharing love.

She, in turn, lathered his body with the sponge over his back and down his chest to his flat stomach. She felt his fresh firmness and was ready for him. He surprised her, twirled her around and began shampooing her hair. The tips of his fingers massaging her scalp gradually restrained her rapid breathing. He rinsed her hair, and then stepped out of the bath, dried himself and put on a navy towelling robe.

"When you're ready, my love." He pointed to a large blue bath towel and white robe hanging on the door. "There's no hurry."

"Umm," she murmured lazily as she watched him walk out into the other room.

He didn't have to wait long before she emerged clad in the robe. She went to sit beside him on the sofa.

"Did you enjoy?" he asked, one brow raised.

"It was the best," she purred. "The best I've ever had."

He shot her an intriguing look.

"The best bath," she replied quickly, suppressing his obvious misinterpretation.

"I wonder!" he teased her as he gently began drying her hair with a soft towel.

She sat still as he tenderly combed it through and left her feeling pampered.

"I wonder," he repeated slowly. "Will you ever reveal your true self to me? I want to know everything about you. I want to delve into your thoughts."

She giggled uncomfortably. "Then I would hold no interest for you. My power lies in my hidden secrets," she quipped flirtatiously. She tilted her head back towards him and added, "If you're honest."

He turned her around to face him. "I would love to penetrate that enigmatic mind of yours. I bet I could hypnotise you."

"No – you couldn't. My mind is too strong. I would never be that weak." She stared adamantly at him. These mind games were getting ridiculous.

He reached for his Saint Christopher on the side and began swinging it like a pendulum. "I bet I could," he said half jokingly.

"Rubbish!" she retorted. Her eyes followed the pendant back and forth. She laughed inwardly.

"Breath deeply," he said softly. "Your mind is blank – you will respond only to my voice – you cannot lie – you will tell the truth."

She did as he said, clearing her mind and concentrating on his voice. Her face grew expressionless.

He counted down from ten to one. He began by warming her up. "Where do you live?"

"Old Moorstone Farm." Her eyes were fixed on the pendulum.

"Good." He was surprised how easy it was. "What are you doing there?"

"Working."

"What are you doing in Cornwall?"

"Having the time of my life."

"What are you running away from?" He was getting excited now.

"The city – London."

"Do you have a lover there?"

"No." Her robe slipped off her silken shoulder, revealing the soft flesh of one breast. Her full lips parted.

He brushed her nipple with his fingertips and witnessed the hardening. Why was he wasting his questions?

"Undo your gown," he ordered.

Slowly she obeyed and the robe slid away from her body.

"Now undo my robe – kiss me."

She did as he told her and kissed his chest.

"Massage my feet Naida," he said, stretching out onto the sofa. "My ankles, my calves – work your way up with your sweet lips."

She did better than that. She licked him all over into such a fever that he was completely distracted from his intended line of questioning.

She then gently led his hands to her own pleasure zones, until they could hold back no longer. She was at the point of no return. He ordered her on top of him and in a matter of seconds, exploded inside her.

"That was incredible," she said.

"Awesome," he murmured dreamily, and then raised his head sharply. "I thought you were under my spell?"

A humorous smile twisted her lips. "Oh but I was darling."

He looked at her with suspicion. Had she manipulated him? His questions had still not been answered. He was none the wiser about her. However, the warmth of her body snuggling close to him made him feel good. He closed his eyes. It all seemed unimportant now.

When Naida awoke, the room was dark. She wondered where she was for a moment, and then felt the sofa cushions beneath her head. The towelling robe was laid across her. Raising her head, she scanned the room for Howard. She heard the sound of cups clinking in the kitchen, just as the antique clock struck one a.m. She sat up naked. The night was still warm.

"I can't sleep any longer," said Howard, walking in with two mugs. "We've been asleep from late afternoon and all evening until now. I've made some coffee."

Naida stretched her arms above her head in the dim light. "That should wake me up – thanks." She yawned and took the cup from him.

He lit two candles and sat in the chair opposite her, so he could see her. The contours of her body, outlined in the glow, generated heat. He fancied he would burn if he touched her. The words – spontaneous combustion – sprang to his mind. He should have sent her home earlier, and then he wouldn't be torturing himself all night with desire for her.

It was as if he couldn't look at her without having to make love to her. He took a last sip of his coffee. What the hell… This time he would not be so premature. The penetration would last long and slow. Impatience was his problem. He must dampen his arousal.

"Let's go for a swim," he said suddenly.

"What now?" she asked surprised.

He stood up and took her hand. "Have you never been night swimming? You've never lived until you have."

"No – I haven't got my bikini." She looked worried. What on earth was he thinking of?

He laughed and pulled her to the door. "You must let go of these inhibitions Naida. The beach will be empty."

This afternoon she thought she had rid herself of all her inhibitions. Why was she hesitating? Why indeed?

He ran out naked across the garden and down to the beach. She followed, warily at first. When she was sure they were completely alone she relaxed.

She watched him run into the waves and disappear. Slowly she eased herself into the sea up to her neck. Enjoying the novelty of swimming by moonlight, she felt an exhilarating sense of freedom in her nakedness. She looked around for him. Where had he got to now? She had no wish to return to the beach naked and alone. If they were together, somehow she would feel safe.

One minute she was nervously combing the water for a sign of him. The next she was rising like Venus from the waves; suspended in mid air for anyone who might happen to see her. Before she registered what was happening, she plummeted back down reaching out to limit her fall, her fingers found Howard's shoulders. He laughed at her surprise.

"What are you doing?" She wound her legs around his waist. "Don't do that to me."

"I couldn't resist it. You looked so lost," he teased as he squeezed her buttocks.

She slid her legs down and felt his hardness rise between her thighs. "No you don't," she giggled, "not after that trick." She prized herself away and dived to escape.

His taut, athletic body was no match for her. He caught her around her waist and let his lips find hers. All the time he was aware that the games she was playing would cause him to become too excited too quickly.

"I know what you want – but I don't think I should let you." She wriggled provocatively against his body, just enough to drive him wild.

He parted her thighs and drew them apart. "You minx, you know only too well what you are doing," he accused her urgently. Then, while she pretended to protest, he thrust into her unfathomable depths. This was not how he intended it to be. He felt his sap rise and about to overflow. With logical effort, he withdrew and left her panting.

"No – no," she moaned. But he knew what he was doing also.

"Cool it – you tantalize me too much," he growled. "It's over too soon. I'll show you how it can be."

He swam away from her to the shore and walked slowly up the beach. She caught him up and flicked the water from her hair onto his back. He spun round and attempted to grab her by the arm. Slipping out of his reach, she watched him with wild eyes, ready to flee or fight. He had ignited her fire and she felt the flame had been doused in petrol.

"Don't tempt me," he said, taking a step towards her.

"I wouldn't dream of it," she answered pertly. She took a step back and raised her hand as if to strike him.

He caught her by the wrists and held them tightly to his chest. "Don't even think of it."

"That's not fair," she shrieked. "You're using brute strength."

"It's as fair as you using your feminine guile to drive me to distraction," he countered.

She struggled against his hold. They looked at each other and were suddenly conscious of the comedy of their situation. He started to laugh first. With a wicked gleam in her eye, she suppressed a giggle. Then she laughed until she thought she would burst, making it difficult for her to keep control as he wrestled her to the sand.

As he bent over her and pinned her arms to the ground, she stopped struggling. Her knees bent to her chest in self defence.

"I've got you where I want you now," he grinned broadly.

She giggled as he tickled her breasts with his tongue. "And you think I belong beneath you?"

It was just beginning to get light before dawn. There would be plenty of time before any early morning swimmers arrived, reasoned Howard. His arousal slowly rose to her teasing. There was no need for foreplay. He drew her knees apart and gently mounted her. "This is worth waiting for," he sighed.

He made her want to abandon herself to pleasure – act out her fantasies. She recalled with a smile how it was on the chair, on the sofa, in the water and now on the sand. He thrilled her with his sense of spontaneity. It was such an adventure, an evocative journey to the sublime realms of her soul. Each thrust was tender, memorable, and immensely enjoyable. They should have done it in the bath!

Arching her back, she returned the thrust to give him deeper access. Her thoughts toyed with the idea of pushing him off in revenge for leaving her gasping in the water. But she knew she could not stop now even if there was an earthquake! Instead

191

she rolled on top of him and found her own rhythm while he worshipped her breasts.

He rolled her back down. His stamina was all he had hoped for. His pleasure was exploring every facet of her. As he extended his rhythm he opened a wide, copious river of emotions. Evocative sounds escaped Naida's lips. He covered them with his own, her breasts rising and falling beneath his hands.

The exaltation in her eyes told him she was on the brink. He felt the sudden rush overtake him. Vibrant percussions spiralled in his imagination.

Chapter 18

Monday evening Naida was relaxing on the bench in the courtyard beneath her window. She had gone about the days work in a hazy dream. After Friday spent with Howard in wicked euphoria on the beach, they had gone back into the cottage, closed the curtains and stayed in bed till Monday. With reluctance they had both left early morning for work.

The hectic weekend and busy work day had finally caught up with her. She let the heady scent of honeysuckle, trailing along the trellis drift over her. The hard wooden seat now replaced the cloud she had been sitting on all day. Gradually she had returned to earth. She became aware of her surroundings. The farmhouse windows were wide open. The evening was sultry and as she let her gaze wander upwards, she noticed the window at the top of the house was the only one shut.

It concerned her. How could Marianne survive in that stifling room? Naida had been so absorbed in her own problems and at the same time indulging in illicit clandestine pleasures, she had completely forgotten Marianne. Nobody else had seemed to have bothered to coax her down lately either. A pang of guilt urged Naida to go up and see her.

As she reached Marianne's door, Naida heard her softly humming. She knocked lightly and immediately the humming stopped.

"Marianne - it's only me – Naida," she called out and waited.

First the footsteps across the room, and then the door handle creaked. Marianne peeked out nervously. And then she smiled. She looked pleased to see Naida.

Eagerly she opened the door wide. "Come in – I was just doing some embroidery."

The heat hit Naida as she entered. "Why don't you open the window Marianne? It's so hot!"

"No – my soul could escape," she said with an air of detachment.

Naida looked astonished and wondered who had put that idea in her head.

"Why should that happen? I open my window when it's hot – so does Ivor and Lowenna," she said brightly. "We still have our souls."

Marianne stopped and stared at Naida. "But I'm different – I know too much. I'm like Lilith. She lost her soul one night and her window was only open a crack."

"Who told you that?" asked Naida.

Marianne bowed her head.

"It's alright – you don't have to tell me." Naida reached out and touched her arm. "Can we sit down?"

"Yes." Marianne removed her sewing from the small sofa.

"So," ventured Naida. "What are you sewing now? Have you finished the tapestry?"

"Not quite." Marianne glanced anxiously at her intricate work. "It must be finished in time."

Naida could feel Marianne tense beside her. "In time for what? Has it something to do with that night you told me about – when you couldn't sleep?"

Marianne clutched the arm of the sofa. The heat was intolerable. She started to feel dizzy.

"You must open the window or you'll faint." Naida walked over and unhooked the catch. "I assure you no harm will come to you."

"Please – no," gasped Marianne, her hands shielding her eyes.

Naida opened the window wide and breathed in the fresh air. "There - that's better." She looked back at Marianne recoiling fearfully in the corner. "See – we are still here – nothing bad has happened and the room feels a lot healthier."

Slowly Marianne withdrew her hands from her face and stood up. Hesitantly, she crept across to the window and expelled the stale air from her lungs, before taking in a deep breath. She could smell the lavender and lilac bushes in the courtyard, mingling with the honeysuckle. She looked out over the fields, sweeping wide their shades of green in the balmy evening, so restful to the spirit. A sigh escaped from her lips in surrender to this revelation.

Naida watched her, hardly daring to breath.

"You've got to stop them!" Marianne suddenly swung round to face her. The words came tumbling out. "They are going to hold a ceremony on the solstice."

"What?"

"Something bad is going to happen." Marianne's brow creased in a worried frown, but the helpless fear in her eyes had gone.

Naida sensed a breakthrough. Perhaps there was hope. "Tell me where it is and what's planned."

"At the ancient disused church in the woods." Marianne shook her head. "I know – I saw what happened a year ago but – I can't remember."

Naida grabbed Marianne's hands. "Try Marianne – try."

"I can't – I can't." Marianne twisted away and sat down on the sofa and put her head in her hands.

Naida construed it must have been so awful that Marianne had blanked it from her mind. "Is – is it something to do with the tapestry?"

"Yes," Marianne glanced with distaste at the gleaming frame against the wall. "They said I knew too much. Then they told me about Lilith."

Naida sat down beside her and said gently. "It's not true what they told you Marianne. I'm sure it's not true."

"She wouldn't join the coven, you see," stated Marianne.

"Nobody knows that," Naida attempted to be rational. "It was over a hundred years ago. These wicked people make things up to suit themselves."

Marianne shook her head. "You don't know what goes on. There are dark secrets in these parts."

Naida shivered and was tempted to close the window. She stood up, went across the room and looked out. All was peaceful. She mustn't let Marianne's ramblings influence her. Marianne had clearly been brainwashed.

"Is it that they wanted you to join?" Naida asked quietly, still looking out over the fields.

"Yes – but I wouldn't," whispered Marianne with a hint of defiance. "Just like Lilith."

Naida glance back over her shoulder. "So you reckon you saw something – and then they saw you?"

"She saw me – I was halfway through the woods." Marianne looked up sharply. "Yes – there was something about to happen. I don't know what – but I think I ran then – I couldn't watch…"

Naida turned round and walked back towards the sofa. "Who was the woman who caught you?"

Marianne stiffened. "She told them. They said I had to join."

"But you didn't?" Naida waited for the denial.

"No," Marianne said guardedly. "I compromised."

Naida realised to pry further and expect Marianne to name her tormentors was unrealistic.

"And this compromise means sewing tapestries for them? They have turned you into a virtual prisoner." Angrily, Naida took the scissors from the table. "I will cut this tapestry to pieces."

Marianne jumped up to restrain her. "No – I have to present it to the church – otherwise I shall live in fear for the rest of my life. Once I have done what they ask I will no longer be beholden to them."

"Oh Marianne." Naida dropped the scissors. "Can't you see it is they that live in fear of you? All you have to do is report them to the police."

"I can't do that." She grabbed Naida by the arm and pleaded. "You won't tell the police, will you? Please don't!"

"I have to Marianne; they are ruining your life. You'll never be free of them. They are destroying your health." Naida tried desperately to make her see sense.

Marianne threw herself back on the sofa. "No – I beg you. You don't know what you are doing," she wailed. "All hell will be unleashed – the serpent will rise."

Naida tried to placate her. "Okay – calm down. I'll not say anything until you're ready. But please don't take the tapestry to the church. I'll think of something. You mustn't involve yourself in any way."

"Thank you," Marianne said with relief. She sank into the cushions completely exhausted.

Naida poured her a drink of water from the jug on the beside table. "While its hot you promise me you will keep the window open – don't be afraid anymore?"

Marianne sipped the water and the colour came back to her cheeks. She smiled. "The roof of the world hasn't caved in, has it? I feel like a demon has been lifted from my shoulders. You are kind."

Naida suppressed a giggle. Marianne said the strangest things. "You don't have to stay up in this room either. Just be sure to come downstairs whenever you like."

"I almost feel I can," said Marianne. "You're my only friend."

Naida wondered why she said that. Ivor and Tom cared for her very much, and Mrs Dunn held her in high esteem. And Lowenna...? Naida looked thoughtful. Well, Lowenna was a handful...

"Ivor and Tom come to see you - don't they?" she asked.

"Sometimes – but Ivor is so busy – I can't expect him often," explained Marianne, looking down. "And Tom finds these stairs difficult."

"But Ivor is your husband." Naida searched Marianne's face. Was she hiding something?"

"It's my own fault – I choose to be alone." Marianne raised her chin. Her expression was convincing.

Naida saw through the brave act. But she couldn't accept that Ivor would abandon his wife. "I'm sure Ivor wouldn't neglect you." Then the unthinkable crossed her mind. "Does he know what's going on?"

"Of course he doesn't – and he mustn't know. It's too dangerous."

Naida wrung her hands in exasperation. "This is all so stupid Marianne. Why suffer in silence?"

"There's more…" Marianne paused and clenched her fists. "No – you don't know what they can do."

"We can't let them win," stressed Naida. She was beginning to feel drained of energy. This house held so many secrets and she had brought her own secrets here too. What a tangled web.

It was beginning to get dark. Marianne got up, restless. "I think we should close the curtains now," she suggested. She looked like a naughty child when she added, "I could – keep the window open."

"You could." Naida raised her eyebrows and smiled and joined Marianne at the window.

They both leant on the windowsill and looked out at the setting sun. The courtyard was still. Naida let her gaze wander across the farm to the outbuildings. The woods were darkening in the distance. In the daytime they were vibrant and alive. Now they appeared remote.

"We used to take Lowenna and Howard for picnics over there," Marianne reflected softly.

Naida followed her wistful gaze to the far fields and tried to picture the family scene. "It must have been a great place for children to grow up. They were lucky."

"Yes – we were happy once," Marianne said sadly and wiped away a stray tear. She shook her head to compose herself. "Sorry – I am being silly."

"I think you are very brave – and you deserve better." Naida consoled her and wondered how these people could live in the same house and be so blind.

"I'm not sure when my life started to crumble," remarked Marianne. "Time distorts – images flow into one another. I get confused," she laughed softly. "I remember how it used to be – up at dawn, days working on the farm until dusk – weekends on the beach with Lowenna and Howard. How they loved it."

"Howard has asked me to marry him," confessed Naida on impulse. It seemed natural to confide in Marianne.

"Yes I wondered," Marianne said brightly. "Lowenna mentioned it was possible and I gather she was none too pleased."

"Oh – I got the impression she would accept it now?" Naida said surprised.

"You never can tell what she's thinking," Marianne turned to Naida. "I'm so pleased – you're perfect for him. I was beginning to wonder if he would ever meet a girl who would be special to him. Every girl so far has fallen short. He doesn't suffer fools gladly. He is a principled man and can't abide dishonesty. There was a girl he was quite keen on but she turned out to be shallow and was anything but honest..." Marianne trailed off. Her attention wandered back to the fields.

Naida swallowed, "Couldn't he find it in him to forgive her?"

"Forgive?" Marianne explored the word with her tongue. "How could he forgive – he couldn't trust her again. They couldn't communicate on the same level." She observed Naida. "Now you – you're good. I doubt if you are capable of telling a lie." It's not in your nature. I'm sure he knows you will never let him down."

Chapter 19

"You're going away?" Naida stopped what she was doing and spun round to face Howard. "What do you mean – where?"

Howard strolled across the kitchen and slid an arm around her waist. "Cool it – I'll only be away until Friday. It's just a short fishing trip." He nuzzled her ear. "Hey – I got a good reaction though, didn't I? You're going to miss me then?"

Naida turned back to the sink and said primly, "I guess I'll survive. At least I won't have to wash your dirty dishes."

"There's gratitude!" Howard picked up the tea towel and waved it in despair. "I cook the lovely lady a wonderful meal and she complains about doing a little washing up!"

Naida looked at him and laughed. "If I didn't know you better I'd swear that's why you asked me here." She tried to adopt a serious expression. "I suppose I'm on trial to see how well I fit into your kitchen. I presume that's where you expect your wife to spend most of her time."

"Of course," he agreed. "Barefoot in the kitchen - with a dozen children around her ankles."

"You must be joking," Naida snorted. "You had better think again."

He laughed throatily. "So – you will be my wife then?"

She shot him a withering glance.

"Okay – okay – I get the message. Hey – I'll tell you why I enticed you here." He put down the tea cloth. "Leave that." He began kissing her neck and running his hands down her curves, accentuated by her cream crochet dress. "I want to make love to you over the sink." He started to stroke her thighs...

She giggled and took a sharp intake of breath. "Howard – you're insatiable."

He was pleasantly surprised to discover she wasn't wearing underwear on this sultry warm evening. "I won't see you for three days!" he murmured huskily, dipping his tongue inside her ear. "Would you prefer the table?"

But it was too late. They couldn't wait. By the time she had wriggled out of her dress, he'd unfastened his jeans…

To end the evening, Howard brewed some coffee. He had to leave early next morning for his trip to Amsterdam.

"I'll think of you at the crack of dawn, while I'm still snuggled up in bed," said Naida, watching him pour the dark liquid into the cups. She curled up on the sofa like a kitten and purred, "Poor Howard."

"Don't pity me." He turned and smiled at her. "There's nothing so beautiful as the onset of first light over the ocean," he sighed. "It's magical."

"I wish I could share it with you," she said whimsically, and then pouted, "I'm going to miss you."

He set the cups down on the table and sat down beside her. "I'll be back before you know it. I return Midsummer Eve. If I'm home in time we can take a stroll in the woods," he winked. "There's an old custom for lovers to frolic in the forest on the Solstice."

"Frolic in the forest?" she laughed at his droll choice of words.

"It's true," he reprimanded her. "In folklore on the solar celebration, young lovers must dance the sacred dance barefoot to absorb the earth's energies, through the labyrinth. Then the life force of the forest will keep their love alive"

She smiled, "Interesting," she said. "Variety can spice up one's love life."

He leaned across and took a small box from the table. "We must never let the flame die. I hope we shall still be making love in the sea and in the woods when our children have flown the nest."

She giggled, "Passionate pensioners!"

He looked affronted. "Don't mock. It's no joking matter. You must be aware of the high divorce rate these days – well, it won't happen to us. I want our love to last till death us do part." He opened the intricate box. "To show you how much you mean to me, I want you to have this Celtic cross – a symbol of my love."

Naida held it in her palm and felt it was carved from a flat pebble. She ran her fingers over the inter-laced knot-work patterns with their unbroken lines. "It's a work of art," she said and wondered if he would love her so much if he knew she had not been completely honest with him.

"See the thread of life. Unravel the cord and rid yourself of your past – of anything that doesn't serve you anymore," he said, placing his hand over

204

hers. "It will lead you on with courage to achieve your goal."

"I've seen this Celtic artwork in the gift shops," she enthused. "It's beautiful."

"It stems from the Druid religion – inherited by the Celtic people," he informed her with pride.

"The Druids? I don't know much about them," said Naida, suspicious that they may have something to do with Marianne. She was tempted to confide in him, but something held her back.

"I will have to teach you sometime," he said, and then grinned. "Initiate you in our secret traditions."

"Sounds ominous." He seemed well informed on the subject. "Is it wise? Some things are best left secret, don't you think?"

"Perhaps," he compromised. "However, I do have something important to tell you. I know I promised not to pester you again for an answer to my proposal… But it's not long till the end of the month, and I have had an unexpected offer."

"Not another marriage proposal?" she quipped. "And you have to make a choice?"

"No – I'm serious Naida," he sighed. "You see, I've been offered a year's work with a fishing firm in America – and if your answer is no… I shall accept."

A chill swept through Naida. She cleared her throat and asked meekly. "What about the seals? Who will care for them?"

"I will leave Blake in charge in my absence." He informed her. "I just hope it doesn't come to this. Naida you must decide what you are going to do by Midsummer Eve on my return."

She nodded, unwilling to look him straight in the eye for fear of betraying her thoughts. "You shall have your answer," she said quietly.

Naida did her work mechanically. Time passed in a daze. Her mind was elsewhere. Soon she would give Howard her answer to his ultimatum. But first she knew she must confront her problems, however daunting.

In the early evening, the house was still and silent with a cool air about it. Naida was sitting on the courtyard bench. Most of the side wall was now enclosed in deep shadow. Ivor and Tom had gone to the Fisheries Inn and Naida had declined their offer to accompany them. She wanted to be alone. In thoughtful mood, she followed the trail of ivy climbing up the stonework. Marianne's window was half open and this pleased her. The only sound was birdsong and all was well.

After agonising over her predicament, she decided it was time to reveal her secret. She felt strangely calm, despite being unsure of the reaction she would receive.

Howard was due back tomorrow and it would all be over by then. She anticipated her joy of accepting his proposal.

"Mrs Naida Elliot," she savoured the words aloud. It sounded perfect. Her future was looking good. Just think no more deceit. Also she would have to stand up to Petros and refuse to be blackmailed. If she informed Sergeant Eames he and his men would give them all protection. She would have to be brave, she couldn't hide forever.

She would never have to see the Batis men again. Her life with Howard would be a loving, supportive partnership. She knew now she had been wrong to think she had to protect Howard. Now she knew him so well, he had more strength of character than any of the Batis men. She could hardly wait for him to return.

By the following morning Naida was ready to approach Ivor with her story. All night she had mulled over how to begin. Anxiety now replaced yesterday's optimism. At breakfast Naida toyed with her cereal. Her nervousness was showing.

"What's up love?" said Mrs Dunn. "You not hungry, then?"

Naida jumped out of her thoughts. "Err - no not really."

Mrs Dunn smiled. "Penny for 'em. I bet you are thinking of your Howard coming home today. I can see you've missed 'im."

"Now you mention it – yes I have."

"Ah now, that's a fact," went on Mrs Dunn. "Then there you go again, absence makes the heart grow fonder."

"You're right Mrs Dunn, it does," agreed Naida. "I wonder what time he will arrive."

Mrs Dunn pursed her lips, tea pot in mid air. "Hard to say with fishermen. There's no set schedule you see – all depends on the job in hand. He could be early or he could get held up in Amsterdam."

Naida hoped he wouldn't be too early. She was sure he meant to be home this evening. She was counting on it so there would be time for her to sort things out. Still, she had better get a move on. Panic made her eat her breakfast hastily.

"There's no rush my girl," said Mrs Dunn, always ready with sensible advice. "When Howard returns you should keep 'im waiting. That way you'll keep 'im on his toes."

"There's something important I have to do before he gets back." Naida drained her tea cup. "I'll see you later." She got up and hurried out to find Ivor.

To her consternation the smallholding was packed with customers. Ivor looked relieved to see her.

"I didn't expect it to be this busy till high season in July," he told Naida, as she helped him serve. "I'm sorry but it looks like you'll not get any respite today. Once the rush starts there's no stopping. Good for business though."

"It's okay," said Naida obligingly. "It'll make the time pass quickly." Although she had been warned of the busy season, she hadn't bargained for it today.

"Oh yes," grinned Ivor. "Howard comes home this evening."

"Yes," replied Naida with a hint of reproach. Why did everyone assume that was all she was waiting for?

The Tregartha's and Mrs Dunn had taken a great interest in their romance and had assured Naida of their approval. This held some consolation. However, by the end of the day she had not managed to talk with Ivor. Wearily she climbed the stairs to her room. The day had been pleasantly chaotic but she was exhausted. She sat on the bed and sighed. Howard had not arrived home yet. For this she was thankful. Perhaps he would be held up until tomorrow and it would give her more time.

On this balmy Midsummer eve, Naida's window was flung wide open. She hardly had the energy to get ready for bed. She lay down and drifted off. It was one minute to midnight when something made her wake up. She noticed the sky was lit faintly by a strange glow. Curious, she got up and went to the window to see where it was coming from. Tall flames were visible in the distance, from the direction of the densely wooded area.

Surely the woods were not on fire, she thought with concern? No, the old church was over there. Suddenly she remembered her conversation with Marianne. Oh my God, something was about to take place tonight. Adrenalin pumped through her veins as she rushed out of her room, down the stairs and through the back door.

It was pitch black as she ran across the fields. She wished she had brought a torch to guide her. The way ahead was hidden by the dark sky, covering her route like a blanket. She stumbled on wondering if the flames had been doused. Then as she came into the wood, she saw them leap up again, as tall as the tallest tree.

Silent as a deer, she crept nearer to find their source. As she came to the clearing, her suspicions were confirmed. The fire had taken hold of the disused church. She was about to run back and raise the alarm when she heard an odd choking laugh. Turning back she saw Marianne standing watching the fire. Naida peered from behind a tree. Marianne was holding something in her hands. She raised it into the air and flung it purposefully into the heart of the fire. Even before Naida recognised the jewel patterns leaping to a devil dance in the flames, she knew it was the tapestry.

Naida clutched the jagged bark of the tree trunk in shock. Eyes wide, mouth open in amazement, she waited. Marianne stood stiff as a statue until there was no trace left of the tapestry. When she was satisfied it had ceased to exist she smiled, turned away and disappeared into the thick forest.

The trees loomed like tall ghosts high above Naida's head. Her rapid breathing had returned to normal now. She must get back to raise the alarm before the fire spread. There was no sign of anyone in the church. If there had been, it was too late to save them.

Hurrying back the way she had come, the shrill sound of a fire engine approaching jolted the silence. Naida paused and was tempted to retrace her steps. But there was nothing she could do to help. Had Marianne started the fire, she wondered?

The following morning, to Naida's surprise, Marianne was sitting at the breakfast table. She looked calm and relaxed, as if nothing had happened.

"I'm going for a walk down to the sea later," Marianne announced.

Naida pulled her chair out slowly and sat down, too stunned to answer. Marianne no longer had the haunted expression she always wore.

"That be nice," said Mrs Dunn. "It's a glorious day you know."

Naida glanced from one to the other in undisguised amazement. Mrs Dunn was obviously pleased to see the improvement in Marianne's mental state. She caught Naida's eye and gave her a reproachful look.

"I wish I could join you, but I have to work this morning," said Naida steadily, "and later I have to go into the village." How could she forget? It was her day for meeting Petros.

"Hear about the fire last night, did you?" Mrs Dunn's declaration caused Naida's heart to leap into her throat.

She glanced at Marianne, expecting her to betray her guilt. If Marianne was to blame, she did not look conscience stricken. Infact she looked positively at ease. The lines on her face appeared smoother, not so pronounced, Naida observed curiously. Marianne finished her breakfast and left, informing them that she would be home at lunch time.

Mrs Dunn turned to Naida, "There's talk already this morning in the village. The rumours are rife about the fire in the old church,"

"What rumours?" asked Naida, quickly. Perhaps Mrs Dunn could shed light on the matter.

"Well – I don't want to frighten you, but it's a known fact, but never spoken openly about," continued Mrs Dunn. "People are scared you see. In these parts there are certain covens – some are for the good and practise healing this land. On the other hand some take advantage of their power and break away to control others." Mrs Dunn looked around her to make sure no one was listening and continued in a hushed voice. "They practise a form of dark magic. It is said they perform sacrifices Midsummer Eve. They choose a maiden of virtue. The Grand master has to initiate her. Then, they subdue her with herbs and sacrifice her on an altar covered with a tapestry."

Naida put her hand to her heart to stop her palpitations. "Oh my God, does this still go on?"

"I heard say in past times – but who knows – whether it's just country folks superstitions - but girls have gone missing, yes. Some most probably had run away to the city, of course but…" replied Mrs Dunn. "They are saying in the village that after last night's fire, it won't ever happen again."

Even when Sergeant Eames called to question them around lunch time, Marianne, who had returned from her walk, sat there with a tranquil expression. Naida was reticent with her answers. It wasn't that she lied, but just concealed what she had seen.

"I would like to question Lowenna also," said Sergeant Eames. "I've already spoken to Ivor and Tom."

"She's not here," replied Marianne, "stayed overnight with friends." She gave a weird smile.

Naida swallowed. She went hot and then cold. What if…? Surely not! Marianne wasn't capable of… Not her own daughter?

Sergeant Eames was leaving now. Naida's head was spinning. She could not be part of this conspiracy. She opened her mouth to speak. Too late – he was gone.

Chapter 20

Howard arrived home in the morning. He had anticipated spending the Solstice with Naida and was disappointed to be held up in Amsterdam. However, he had been deliberating seriously over their relationship. The vast endless sea always made him turn inwards and ponder upon his future. He was sure of his love for her. When he was with her the world appeared lit by angels singing her praises. Despite this, he had to admit there was a niggling doubt; a certain mystery that added to her charm… But was she genuine? Before seeing her again, he decided there was something that must take precedence.

He had parked his car at the back of the cottage out of sight. He was waiting just inside the front door when the post arrived. He scanned it quickly. A couple of letters, both junk mail. Damn, he sighed and settled down with the newspaper to wait.

No more letters had arrived. He became impatient, realising he was wasting his time. Perhaps the sender of the poison pen letters, achieving no response, had lost interest. With a mixture of relief and annoyance, he decided to forget the matter. It was probably some jealous nutcase from the village. The boy Mark had come under his suspicions. It had crossed Howard's mind when he remembered how besotted Mark seemed with Naida at the party. However, he had seen him occasionally since, with various pretty girls on his arm. He had not wasted much time and hardly looked broken hearted. No, Mark was eliminated.

He was sure Naida had nothing to hide. She was virtuous in his eyes. She did love him, he reasoned. He must put this nonsense in a logical perspective. With this in mind, he went to make himself lunch.

He was in the middle of preparing a sandwich when he heard the click of the letter box. It wasn't loud but under the circumstances it made him jump. He was through the hall in a flash and immediately recognised the red print on the envelope.

Lowenna was halfway down the path when Howard rushed out of the door. The expression on his face was thunderous.

"So it was you," he bellowed in disbelief.

Lowenna trembled. By the look of him a storm was about to erupt and she could not escape. She contemplated running, but that would be useless. She had been caught red handed.

Instead, she blurted out, "Can't you see Howard! I did it for your own good? Naida doesn't love you; she's using you – using all of us. Her and her fiancé plan to rob Father and go back to London. I know, I've seen them plotting. They meet in the village. I'll take you – I'll show you."

She reminded Howard of an innocent puppy – her large eyes gazing up at him, her fingers innocently twirling a strand of spun gold hair. However, he could not believe her. He knew her too well.

"I should put you over my knee and spank you. How could you do such a wicked thing? How can you tell such lies?" he stormed.

She shook her blonde bob with exasperated denial. Her game wasn't working. "But it's true. I'll take you to them, and then you will believe me."

214

She grabbed his arm. "It's me you belong with Howard – not her. She could never make you happy."

He pushed her away. "What are you saying? You don't know your own mind. Don't you realise what you have done?"

"Just give me a chance," she pleaded. "They meet at three o'clock."

He took hold of her by the wrist with one hand, waving the letter at her with the other. "Let us see what devious lies you have written this time?"

She struggled violently against him. "Leave me alone."

"You little wild cat." He let go of her and ripped open the letter. GO TO THE GATE AT THE EDGE OF THE VILLAGE 3.00 NAIDA MEETS LOVER.

Lowenna had decided that she would have Howard at any cost. Naida would not come between them. Her obsession spurred her on. "She has no intention of marrying you."

"Nonsense! I will not even consider this," raged Howard. He took her by the shoulders and shook her.

This incensed her further. With eyes blazing she kicked out and caught him on the shin.

"Ouch, you little bitch." He rounded on her furious. "Right, you will come inside and wait until I decide what to do with you." He dragged her, protesting, back inside the cottage.

The first hour was spent in stony silence. Howard paced restlessly up and down the room, while Lowenna sat pouting in a sulk. Finally he turned to her.

"Alright," he said, "you come with me to the place they are supposed to meet – and God help you Lowenna when I find out the truth."

Naida paused. She was about to open the door of the land rover. Somehow she felt uneasy about her rendezvous with Petros this afternoon. Maybe it was her intuition. It was as if a voice inside her head was telling her not to go. A premonition!

This was the last time she would meet him. She was going to tell him that she was not going to give in to his demands anymore. Then she would have her talk with Ivor and hope Howard could find it in his heart to forgive her for not telling him the truth from the beginning.

Petros was leaning nonchalantly on the gate as usual. Naida got out of the land rover and walked towards him.

"It's over Petros," she stated firmly. "I will not give you a penny more."

"No problem," he replied lazily. "Father has ordered me to come home. So I must not disappoint him. I am obliged to show him some results of my search for you."

Alarm bells began to ring in Naida's head. "What do you mean?"

"Well what do you think sister? You will come back with me of course. I think your holiday has lasted long enough, don't you?" In case she had other ideas, he took hold of her securely by the shoulders. With his back to the gate he pinioned her against him so she couldn't escape.

At the far end of the field, Howard and Lowenna could just make out the two figures that appeared to be embracing. Naida struggled to free herself. She swung her head away, her unmistakable hair glinting in the sun.

"I have kept my part of the bargain," she cried, "Enough is enough – why can't you honour yours?"

"Bargains are made to be broken," jeered Petros. "Anyway, you were about to break your part of the bargain."

"Blackmail you mean," she snapped. "I should have known better!" She tried desperately to resist as he pushed her forcefully towards his car.

To Howard, from a distance, the ensuing struggle looked compromising. "I have seen enough," he aid acidly.

Lowenna was triumphant. "What did I tell you?"

Howard stumbled back to his car. He slumped onto the seat and put his head in his hands. "What a fool I've been," he mumbled and did now assume that Naida had been trifling with his affections. His first impression had been right after all. "How could she?"

Lowennas victory gave her courage. "I knew she was no good the moment I laid eyes on her. I never trusted her. Everyone else was taken in by her sly, cunning ways." She put a consoling hand on his arm. "Don't blame yourself Howard. Now you can forget her and we can plan our future together."

"Don't be ridiculous," he shook his head and banged his fist on the steering wheel. "You still don't realise what you've done, you stupid little fool. Just - just go home Lowenna. Leave me alone."

She knew he meant it. "Alright, but you wait - you'll want me one of these days and I won't be around. You will have missed your chance," she screamed, her voice rising in crescendo. A woman scorned!

Naida contemplated jumping from the car on the busy motorway. A quick glance down at the road, speeding by at an alarming rate, changed her mind. Nonetheless, perhaps it would solve everything, she thought wryly.

Petros's face was set in grim determination. Naida's heart sank as she sat in silent contempt. Through villages, and then towns, the passing hours took her further away from security and nearer her peril.

After the tranquillity of Cornwall, the overcrowded streets of London attacked her senses violently. She had become attuned to the gentler, rural way of life where she knew she belonged. The late shoppers milling in the centre of the city swarmed like ants, rushing to and fro. The noise was deafening. Music blaring out from an open doorway, the sound of raised voices, the hooting of impatient drivers, all contributed to her unease.

It reminded her of the rush hour on the underground and packed tube trains. Everybody going about their business single-mindedly –

dispassionately. She could not come back to this. The traffic lights turned red and a gang of punks ran passed her nightmare, shouting obscenities at Petros through the open car window. He countered back with a string of expletives.

Naida's heart began to beat rapidly. Petros wound up the window. The lights changed to green and the heavy traffic started moving again. The car crawled along agonisingly slow. A few turnings later she was back in familiar territory, outside the old Victorian house. The grey pavements and buildings of London always reminded her of the pigeons in Trafalgar Square, rain and puddles.

In her teens it had all been so exciting. Life was new and experimental. It was great to be in the centre – the hub of things. Now it all seemed like a lifetime ago. These things were no longer important. She'd had time to reflect and discover what she really wanted, and at this moment she had never been so sure.

The house meant nothing to her now her Mother wasn't there. It felt austere – empty. Her stepfather's face was hard as granite. He looked a formidable character as he glared down at her.

"Ah – so the wanderer returns," he stated coldly.

Her lips trembled. She stood her ground. Courage came from the anger inside her. "Not by choice," she replied bravely.

"Hmm – you always were a spirited girl. Perhaps we can teach you some obedience and to respect our customs. Where have you been?" he demanded. "Your explanation had better be good."

She raised her chin defiantly. "I had to get away from this place. You would never allow me to be my own person. I will not be dictated to – I could never marry Rico Pettroulli!" The very thought of such a future gave her strength to defy Andreas. She would not let him think he could control her. "This is not Cyprus – this is England. Women have just as much right to choose as men. We are not chattels for men's convenience," she raged hysterically. "It's the twentieth century or didn't you know, or are you living in a time warp?"

His hand lashed out, catching her sharply across the face. Naida gasped and clutched her cheek.

"How dare you disobey me," he ranted. She noticed the purple veins protruding from his neck. "I will hear no more excuses. Go to your room and stay there. Tomorrow you meet your betrothed."

"No!" she protested.

He nodded to Petros, who then took hold of her arm and ushered her forcefully up the stairs. He pushed her inside the room and shut the door as he left, locking it.

Naida fell into a heap onto the bed and began to sob. Would she ever see her beloved Howard again? There must be a way to escape. Her eyes searched the room. She got up and tried the window, but found it securely locked.

Presently, the door opened and Petros brought in a tray of food. "Eat this sister, for tomorrow is your big day," he taunted," and you must keep your strength up." He laughed and left her alone once more.

Her appetite was none existent. Her mouth was dry so she drank the cool lemonade and left the rest. Tired and weary from the journey, she eventually fell into a fitful sleep. Nightmares haunted her. Clearly she saw Howard sailing far away over the horizon. A girl with golden hair tipped him over the edge. Psyche appeared sitting on a high rock gazing into the distance surrounded by sea. Aphrodite confronted her. With a sense of inevitability she awaited her death in the jaws of the monster lurking in the murky depths. Far away, Eros disappeared in the sky, like a leaf in the wind.

Naida awoke with a sense of impending doom, as if there was no hope and no one would know of her predicament. The key turned in the lock. Andreas stood in the doorway holding a dress and shoes.

I want you to have a shower and then put these on," he ordered, "our guests will be arriving shortly."

"No – I will not," she protested mutinously.

Very well, if you are going to continue to behave immaturely, I shall treat you like a child and put it on for you myself." He came towards her. She shrank away, and then snatched the dress from him, throwing it onto the bed.

That's better – now go and have your shower," he said.

In a daze, Naida went to the adjoining bathroom. Perhaps she would feel fresher after a shower. It would clear her head, and anyway arguing would achieve nothing. She must play for time.

Stepping out of the bathroom Naida reluctantly picked up the dress and put it on, knowing only too well that Andreas did not make idle threats. The black garment accentuated her curves. The top and sleeves were sheer antique lace, which left nothing to the imagination. How could Andreas make her wear this? She supposed it was to impress Rico Pettroulli. In a desperate attempt to look dowdy, she scraped back her hair and tied it severely at the nape of her neck. She had no intention of applying any makeup. Little did she realise there was no way she could make herself look plain.

Andreas entered her room and surveyed his prize possession. "Perfect Chiquita. I'm glad you have come to your senses." He gave a superior smile. "A picture of innocence. Just a hint of lipstick I think and you will capture his heart."

"I have none," she stated blankly.

"No? Let us see." He opened her bag. "Ah – what's this then?" He held up a deep red lipstick in a silver case.

She glowered at him though the mirror as he stood over her, making sure she applied the gloss to her lips. He then opened a velvet box, producing a gold locket and heart shaped earrings. This time he fastened the necklace around her neck himself.

"Put on the shoes – then I will escort you downstairs. I am sure you are eager to meet your future husband. He is a man who will keep us all in luxury and raise our family's status," he said arrogantly.

Naida did not trust herself to pass comment. As if in a bad dream, she allowed herself to be taken downstairs. Andreas paused at the bottom to pluck a deep red rose from a tall vase and fixed it in her hair. She felt strange, as if she, the person, did not exist – had no part in this bizarre pageant. If she pinched herself she would wake up and find herself transported back into the protective surroundings of Old Moorstone farm.

The room was full of her stepfather's Greek Cypriot friends. Some she recognised and nodded politely. Andreas steered her towards Rico Pettroulli, standing expectantly, almost obscured by a large rubber plant. Naida felt dizzy and suppressed an incongruous urge to laugh out loud at the sight of this pompous little rotund, balding man. He reached out to take her hand in his. She immediately withdrew it from his clammy palms.

"At last Naida – you are a vision." He leered down her cleavage.

Naida didn't answer for the fear of being physically sick. Andreas proceeded to discuss a few minor details with Rico about the wedding, completely ignoring Naida.

"I will leave you two alone to get acquainted. I am sure you can come to an amicable agreement and set a date," Andreas said finally, before walking over to Petros.

"Watch her," he whispered unobtrusively. "I want nothing to stop this marriage."

"Don't worry; she will not cause us any trouble. I know how to deal with her," answered Petros.

Naida steadied herself against the wall. "I feel faint," she uttered.

"Come and sit down – take my arm," suggested Rico.

She felt him undress her with his eyes. "No, I will be fine in a minute. I need some fresh air. I won't be long." She made for the open French windows.

"Good idea, I will accompany you," he answered before she had time to escape.

Naida took a deep breath and sat down resignedly on the patio chair. Rico brought another chair close, breathing heavily into her ear. His eyes devoured her body. He ran his tongue repulsively over his lips and swallowed in anticipation.

"I have waited so long for you Naida. I can give you anything you want. You will live like a princess."

She turned away in disgust from his garlic breath and caught sight of Petros's reproachful eyes, checking her from inside the house. She scanned the garden. If only Rico would go inside!

"Would you fetch me a glass of water please Rico?" she asked.

"Water may be good for you if you feel unwell," he considered, "but wine might loosen you up. You seem a little tense. I expect it's the excitement. I should like you to relax. We must get to know each other intimately. After all we are to be married and it's only natural I want to be alone with you. I shall come to your room later, discreetly."

Naida turned sharply to face him. "Whatever do you mean?"

"Ah my sweet innocent - don't be alarmed, I am a man of the world and understand your anxiety. I can teach you to enjoy and please me so our honeymoon will be all the more enhanced." His face reddened. He wiped the perspiration from his brow. "You will not be disappointed."

"This is ridiculous – don't be absurd," she retorted. "What if I already have a lover?"

"You have such a sense of humour Naida– I see you like to tease me," He gave her a lecherous smile. "I can see we will have fun."

"I am not joking,"

"Preposterous! You are a Greek girl, are you not?" he asked. "Anyway your Father has vouched for your chastity."

"What if I am not wholly Greek? What if he is not my Father?" she replied coldly.

"It would be an insult for Andreas to lie on such a matter," he bristled with indignation.

Curbing the desire to slap him hard, she arose and ran back inside, hoping to retreat to her room. She found her way barred at the foot of the stairs by Petros.

"Where do you think you are going Chiquita," he snarled.

"Let me by. I want to go upstairs," she shrieked, attempting to push past his immovable thick body,

"Where are your manners? You are supposed to be entertaining Rico," he snapped.

"This is madness – none of you can force me to do this." She stepped back from his solid form filling the stairway.

Rico was hurrying across the room and into the hall. "Whatever is the matter?" he panted.

Naida wondered hopefully if he had a weak heart. A pang of guilt flashed momentarily across her thoughts.

"Naida feels a little ill. Nothing to worry about," answered Petros.

"I want to go to my room," Naida stated firmly, clenching her fists at her sides.

"Yes, I think she should lie down for awhile. She is obviously overcome." Rico said officiously. "I want her to be fresh for later."

"Very well, do as he says," Petros shifted his position.

Naida flew up the stairs and shut the door behind her. She heard Petros turn the key in the lock from outside.

"Don't try any tricks," he said vehemently.

His barbaric, insensitive attitude enraged her. "And what do you get out of this Petros?"

"For a start a house in Cyprus and a share in the Petroulli property empire," he jeered. "Father and I will enjoy a high standard of living – and you too sister, if you play your cards right. I can't see what you're complaining about. Our social standing will be raised. We will be people of importance – able to command respect."

"You insufferable pig. Have you no morals? You sell your own sister for greed," she ranted, incensed with outrage. The lively Greek music coming from the sitting room swallowed their voices.

"Nothing I tell you – nothing will stop us!" he hissed. His evil laugh echoed eerily as he descended the stairs.

He was mad, thought Naida. For that matter, they all were. Surely Rico must realise by now that she had no intention of marrying him. Was the man so thick skinned he hadn't got the message or maybe he

226

would enjoy the power of possessing her against her will. In his arrogance he probably thought once she had spent time alone with him, she would be bowled over. Naida shuddered at the thought. She had to escape or the consequences did not bear thinking about.

The window was still securely locked. Naida scanned the room frantically. The bathroom – yes, she remembered the window was shut, but she had not tried it. To her relief it opened. Without a backward glance, she climbed through onto the ledge. A low flat roof jutted beneath her. Trying to think clearly, logic took over. She would need money for the train fare back to Cornwall and her bag was still on the bed.

Taking a chance, she eased herself back inside. Voices sounded ascending the stairs. She stood rigid and listened, not daring to breath. Whoever it was passed by her door. Naida expelled her breath slowly. She was shaking. It was now or never.

Chapter 21

Not until she had boarded the train did Naida feel safe and begin to relax. She knew, once Andreas had found her missing, he would be enraged and come looking for her. By then, she would be safe with Howard and would have told him everything. The thought of being back in his arms where she belonged kept her going.

The train rumbled on through the city and out into the countryside, past sloping valleys and hedgerows, resplendent with a wealth of wild flowers. Naida must have dozed off for a few hours, for when she awakened it was getting dark. A porter called through the carriages:

"Next stop Falmouth!"

The train screeched to a halt. She alighted at the station and was grateful to catch a bus almost immediately to Peranuthnoe. She walked briskly along the crooked streets, through the peaceful backwater, and then climbed the hillside with its familiar slate-hung cottages lining the sea wall.

Although it was late she was not afraid. Only when Howard's cottage came into view, did she begin to step up her pace – impatient to be with him again. She ran up the path and knocked loudly. The door swung wide.

"You have a nerve coming here." Howard glared at her bitterly.

"What?" Naida gasped, unprepared for this change in him. He was like a stranger. It was as if they had meant nothing to each other.

"Go back to your boyfriend. You have betrayed me," he spat with iron determination. "Look at you – all dressed up. I suppose he likes you to dress like that, does he?"

Naida had forgotten she was still wearing the hideous creation Andreas had forced on her. "But you don't understand."

"On the contrary – I understand only too well. All this time you have been stringing me along - and for what, Naida?"

He hurled her down to the depths of despair with his disdain. She was reminded of the venomous Arachnid.

"Why are you treating me like this?" she shrieked. "You've got it all wrong."

"No doubt amusing yourself at my expense," he continued, unwilling to listen to her explanations. "And to think I was fool enough to fall in love with you. No wonder you would never consent to marry me."

This was crazy. Naida couldn't grasp what he was saying. Her legs began to buckle. She swayed, as if descending down a dark spiral.

"One thing I can never forgive you for is deceiving Marianne into believing you were her friend," he stated icily, "All the time you were using her for your own ends."

"No – no, how can you believe that?" It seemed that since yesterday her life had sunk from bad to worse.

"It's no use Naida; I have the full story from Lowenna. Is it true you are to be married?"

So that was it. Lowenna had finally turned him against her. The girl possessed an evil power. She was obviously still very much alive. Like the phoenix she had risen from the ashes. This eased Naida's conscience somewhat. However her heart felt like lead. She felt numb. How the power of hate can kill, she thought metaphorically. Only the power of love can heal.

"Is that what you believe?" she asked coolly with a sense of resignation.

"Yes," He stood firm, unyielding. "I have seen with my own eyes."

After what she had endured, Naida's patience was over stretched. Furious, adrift in an angry sea, she was drowning. Being walked all over had left her flat. If he wanted to believe a little schemer like Lowenna, he could think what he liked. There was nothing more for her to say. Her refusal to answer one way or the other brought Howard to the conclusion that it must be true.

"I wish you had never come into my life," he stormed. "I never want to set eyes on you again."

"Fine – that's fine by me," she retaliated. She raised her chin – it was his loss. He did not live up to her expectations anyway. The future she had so happily envisaged disintegrated as she watched him close the door on her life.

It was a fair walk back to Old Moorstone Farm. Soon Naida's pace, spurred on by anger, had slowed to a weary trudge. What a fool she had been. If only she hadn't procrastinated and faced the music in the very beginning; then she would have known the score. She had been caught in the net, entangled in her own fear of the consequences.

She could go away – disappear into the night. It would be easy. After all, she doubted the Tregartha's would want her to stay any longer after Lowenna had spun her vindictive lies. But where would she go? Anyway, Andreas and Petros were sure to catch up with her sooner or later. She would forever be looking over her shoulder. There was no way around it – she would have to face the music.

With resignation, she marched up the drive to Old Moorstone Farm. No sooner had she turned her key in the door, when the pitch blackness was lit up, trapping her like a rabbit in the harsh glare of headlights. A figure jumped from the car.

"I will teach you to run off like that." Andreas grabbed her arm and raised a hand in readiness to strike.

Naida screamed, shattering the silence of the sleeping household. Ivor appeared at the door. Andreas hand stopped in mid air. He turned his attention to Ivor.

"So you are the one who has stolen my daughter. My son has informed me that you have been harbouring her."

"What – who on earth…?" began Ivor, astounded. He attempted to register what was happening.

Naida caught the glint of the knife in Petros' hand. She took a sharp intake of breath and opened her mouth to scream. Petros's eyes dilated wildly. He lunged forward, bursting through the door towards Ivor.

"No Petros – no," Naida screamed in terror. "He's my Father."

In that split second, Tom, who had come to Ivor's aid, threw himself across his son. The blade caught Tom in the chest. He staggered awkwardly onto the floor. Naida ran to him, cradling him in her arms. Ivor knocked the knife from Petros's hand. It clattered noisily onto the ground. With one almighty punch, he sent Petros reeling.

Andreas was already in the car, igniting the engine. "You fool Petros," he shouted. "Get in the car."

Petros picked himself up and stumbled over. The car skidded in the earth as Andreas swung it around. Petros hauled himself in.

"We'll be back. There is nowhere you can hide," Andreas called vehemently, before screeching off down the drive in a cloud of dust.

Narrowly, he missed the police car turning in by the gate. Ivor ran out to meet the Sergeant. "They've got away!" he raised his hands in frustration.

Sergeant Eames got out of the car, followed by George. "Marianne phoned us. She reported a break in. We came as quickly as we could."

"Not quick enough," Ivor shot back impatiently.

Naida looked across at Ivor speaking to the policeman, and then back at Tom. A stray tear trickled onto the black lace of her dress. "I'm so sorry," she whispered.

Tom raised his eyes to her. "There now, don't cry m' dear. I should've known – so like your Mother Eleni you are."

232

"Shh, the ambulance will be here soon," soothed Naida. She took his hand.

"It's alright – I'll be fine, you'll see." He winced with pain, and then whispered, "I remember the very day Ivor brought your Mother home to meet us. She was charming."

"Don't Tom, don't. Hush now," urged Naida, and then glanced towards the gate. "I think I hear the ambulance.

Marianne came down the stairs. She had dressed to accompany Tom to the hospital.

"Shall I come too?" asked Naida anxiously. Despite the trauma, Marianne appeared confident - in full control.

"No, you stay with Ivor," she smiled gently.

Naida stood aside, bewildered. Once the ambulance and police car had departed, she faced Ivor. His eyes held sorrow.

"Naida," he said quietly. "Why didn't you tell me?"

She shook her head in despair. "I'm sorry; I've caused so much trouble. If I had known it would lead to this I would never have come searching for you."

"Don't say that." He stepped forward, enfolding her in his arms and rocked her gently. "I am glad I've found a daughter, even if it is a surprise – a pleasant surprise."

She raised her tear stained face.

He looked at her with a sense of wonder. "Mine and Eleni's daughter." He shook his head at the revelation, hardly daring to believe. "If only she had let me know."

"She lived in fear of her family's retaliation," explained Naida. "When they discovered she was pregnant they forced her into an arranged marriage with Andreas. I only found out the truth just before Mother died."

"My dear," said Ivor. "That must have come as a shock."

Naida nodded meekly as she remembered. It had indeed shocked her to discover that Andreas was not her real father. "Mother begged me to forgive her but I assured her I understood."

"So this character that attacked Tom is your half brother," stated Ivor objectively.

"No – he's my stepbrother. When Andreas married my Mother, he was a widower in need of a Mother for his baby son. He was ignorant of the fact that I wasn't his. He evidently thought it was a premature birth." She began to sob quietly. "All my life I believed Andreas was my Father. He was such a cold man – we had nothing in common."

Ivor soothed her, letting her cry for awhile before confiding, "Eleni was the great love of my life, you know."

Naida took a deep shuddering breath and wiped away her tears. "I guessed as much and I think she loved you till the day she died."

He stared wistfully out into the darkness, across the fields. His eyes had a far away look as if he was reliving the days of his youth.

"She was only twenty – so beautiful. I worshipped her. She lit up the room whenever she entered." He spoke distantly, almost to himself, lost in another time only he could enter.

Naida sensed his pain and ached for the past to have turned out differently. "When did you last see her?"

That part of his life he recalled vividly. "I was in London, spending the summer break from college, with friends. Eleni, your Mother, was also on holiday. We met in Hyde Park, where groups of students congregated in those days," he explained. "I noticed her straight away. She was so vibrant, she stood out."

Naida managed a weak smile. "Was it love at first sight?"

"You could say that." He paused, thoughtful. "You know what I remember most about her? Her laughter. Yes – her radiance and her glossy black hair, reaching to her waist. She was such a delicate creature. I was captivated."

"I can't imagine her like that." Naida was surprised at his description of her sombre, dutiful Mother. Circumstances must have made her lose her sparkle.

Ivor sighed. "All too soon the summer ended and I returned to college. Eleni went home to Cyprus. We vowed to write until we could meet again. I wrote so many times. She replied just once. I still have the letter."

Naida felt sad and angry all at once.

"Then she never replied again," continued Ivor. "I assumed she had forgotten me."

"No, that wasn't so," affirmed Naida, resolute. "You have to understand the Greek ways. To save face, which is important for the honour of the family, she was sworn to secrecy about her pregnancy. You can't blame her. She was manipulated."

"I only hope she didn't suffer," he murmured, with regret for what could have been.

The night had turned cool. They wandered inside and sat on the window seat.

Ivor continued. "After college, I married Marianne. We'd known each other from childhood. We were fond of each other. I needed a wife to help run the farm – it was practical."

Naida shrugged resignedly. "It's strange how fate deals the cards."

"Not so strange," he answered philosophically, and then added, "You've been through a lot Naida. Now you have us to help you. Once Tom comes home, we'll put all this behind us."

"He will be alright, won't he?" she asked. "I would never forgive myself…"

Ivor gave a wry smile. "Don't worry; he's a tough old boy. He'll survive," he promised. "And tomorrow I think you will have to pay a visit to Howard and explain a few things, don't you? Nothing would make me happier than to see you two wed."

"I'm not sure he will listen," she sighed. Her heart sank as she recalled her confrontation with Howard.

"I'm sure he'll be pleased when he knows the truth," replied Ivor, unaware of the clash between them.

Naida didn't have the heart to put him straight. She was unsure whether she could cope with another trauma. She also wondered how Marianne would react to the news.

"How is Marianne?" she queried.

"You know, I can't understand it, she's made a remarkable recovery." Ivor shook his head, pleased but perplexed. "I'm worried about Lowenna though. She's become very withdrawn."

Naida looked surprised. "Withdrawn?" she repeated. "Lowenna? Surely not."

"It baffles me too," remarked Ivor. "Marianne says not to worry – it's just another of Lowenna's phases. I suppose she's right." After a brief pause he went on cheerfully. "Marianne and I have been taking long walks together – getting to know each other again."

Naida wondered what was going on. There appeared to be a complete reversal of roles.

"I'm so glad," she smiled. "And where is Lowenna?"

"Staying with a friend," replied Ivor.

Naida blinked. Her eyes felt heavy. She could hardly keep them open.

"You look exhausted," said Ivor. "It's been a long day. We had better get some sleep. You needn't get up early. Its market day tomorrow."

Chapter 22

Early next morning Mrs Dunn came scurrying up the path to Old Moorstone Farm. She looked agitated as she knocked on the door.

"Morning Mrs Dunn," said Ivor. He noticed she appeared flustered. "Anything wrong?"

Mrs Dunn steadied her breathing. "It's Howard," she blurted out. "Mr Tregartha – Howard's gone. Gone away to sea – asked me to deliver this letter to you."

Ivor frowned. Nothing surprised him anymore. "Come in," he said and took the letter with a sense of fatalism.

"*Dear Ivor,*" he read.

"*Forgive me for departing without saying goodbye but I cannot stay any longer. I have to get away. Lowenna told me everything. Although what she did was wrong, in a way she did me a favour – opened my eyes to the truth. I always looked on Lowenna as a little sister, but you know Ivor, you and Marianne have spoilt her. She's headstrong and needs discipline. Don't give her so much freedom. Send her back to school.*

Sadly I must warn you not to trust Naida. Tell her to go. She deceived you like she deceived me. I loved her and my heart is heavy.

I sail for America and I don't know when I shall see you again. Take care and love to Marianne. I shall write when I'm settled.

Your friend always
Howard.

"Oh no!" exclaimed Ivor. He sat down and dropped the letter on the table. "What has Lowenna been saying? It must be a pack of lies." He put his head in his hands, and then raised his eyes to Mrs Dunn. "He's gone to America."

"Yes, I know," she replied. "He came to see me last night on the way to the ship. Well it was the early hours really." She folded her arms. "I wondered who was knocking at such an ungodly hour."

Ivor leaned his head to the side, thoughtful. "Whatever possessed him?" he muttered.

"He gave me the key to his cottage," continued Mrs Dunn, "asked if I'd pop in from time to time and keep an eye on it. Of course I said I would and then he gave me the letter."

"I wish he'd come to see me first," said Ivor with a growing feeling of annoyance. He began tapping his fingers on the table.

Mrs Dunn sighed. "I says – well aren't you going to say your goodbyes to them yourself and he looked thoughtful and says it was best not to. I can't fathom it – and just like that 'e went."

Ivor shut his eyes for a moment and thought of Lowenna. He turned pensively towards the window. Was it their fault she had turned into such a monster? He hoped it wasn't too late to rectify their mistakes.

He turned back to Mrs Dunn. "A lot happened here last night. I would like you to be the first to know, besides the family, I have discovered that Naida is my daughter," he announced proudly.

"Oh my," Mrs Dunn's hand flew to her chest, her heart fluttering. For once she was lost for words.

"Yes, it's true. It's a long story," said Ivor. Then after a moment's reflection added more seriously. "I'm afraid there is some bad news also."

Mrs Dunn put her hand to her mouth in shock as Ivor went on to reveal Tom's

injury. "I can't believe it – it's too much to take in."

"I phoned the hospital this morning. He's weak but improving," Ivor reassured her. "The knife missed his heart, thank God."

"Who did it, I'd like to know?"

"I'll explain it all later," replied Ivor wearily. "You don't have to be concerned."

Mrs Dunn's curiosity was too overwhelming. She persisted. "Has it anything to do with that man seen lurking in the village?"

"Probably - I'm not sure of all the facts yet." Ivor waved a hand dismissively.

Mrs Dunn looked at the clock. "Well, I can't nattter all morning. I've got work to do. But first you 'ad better see these." She searched in her bag and produced some crumpled paper. "I found these screwed up in Howard's waste paper bin this morning."

Ivor took them from her and read them. He shook his head. "Now it all falls into place. This is Lowenna's doing," he said angrily. "I'm going to order her home immediately. She has a lot of explaining to do."

"Well, it's none of my business Mr Tregartha, but I says to myself I could see trouble brewing years

240

ago with young Lowenna." Mrs Dunn pursed her lips, and then confided, "I've known 'er since she was born – she's always 'ad a mind of her own."

"She's gone too far this time," said Ivor in calm judgement. "I'll deal with her."

Naida awoke to the sound of the land rover starting up. She stretched and got out of bed, just in time to catch a glimpse of Ivor driving off to market. She wondered fleetingly why he had gone without her. Then it all came flooding back. Tom! She must find out how he was. She slipped on her robe and walked along the landing, straight into Marianne coming out of the bathroom.

"Marianne – how's Tom?" she enquired urgently.

"He's as well as can be expected," replied Marianne. She bent forward and squeezed Naida's arm. "Don't worry my dear; the doctor says he'll pull through."

Naida glanced down nervously. She wondered what Marianne was thinking after last night's confession. "Thank goodness," she whispered.

"Considering his age, it's a miracle he survived," Marianne stated frankly.

Naida avoided eye contact. This newly confident woman disconcerted her. Nevertheless, Marianne did not act like a woman betrayed.

"Will he be in hospital long?" Naida asked.

Marianne smiled. "Depends how he progresses. Now, freshen up and join me for breakfast."

Naida showered quickly and dressed. As she descended the stairs she prepared herself mentally to face Marianne. However, she need not have worried.

241

Marianne came straight to the point. "You know Naida; there was no reason to fear telling us you are Ivor's daughter. All this could have been avoided if you had confided in the beginning."

A lump came to Naida's throat. "I'm sorry," she found herself apologising again. "I would do anything to turn the clock back. I didn't want to come between you and Ivor."

"Now how could you do that?" Marianne looked at her consolingly. "I've grown very fond of you. I realised when I married Ivor that it wasn't a passionate relationship. Of course we care for each other deeply." She put her hand over Naida's. "I'm glad he once knew great love. I would never deny him that happiness."

Tears pricked Naida's lashes. "Why is life so unfair?"

"Compromise," stated Marianne tactfully. "It's all about compromise. I too loved someone in the past – just a dim memory now that proved impossible. There – I've told you now. You see Naida, for some of us it only happens once in a lifetime."

Naida sat back in her chair, thoughtful. "Do you really believe that?" She hoped it wasn't true because that would mean she would end up a very lonely old woman.

"Sometimes we have to settle for companionship, which isn't a bad thing," answered Marianne.

The idea appalled Naida. She could not envisage settling for such a bland arrangement. It would be anathema to her passionate spirit.

Marianne must have sensed her dismay, for she said, "But if you love someone strongly, as if they

242

are the missing part of your soul, don't let them slip away."

Naida looked at her in despair. "Already it is too late I fear. Howard believes I love someone else and never wants to see me again."

"Tell him it's not true," said Marianne forcefully. "I'm sure he will see sense eventually."

Naida recalled his harsh words and bit her lip. "No, I could never do that. Not after the way he spoke to me." She felt in her heart there was no hope.

"Why not?" Marianne reasoned. "It seems the sensible thing to do. You know how volatile Howard can be. He probably regrets what he said right now."

"The point is – he said it." Naida's hackles rose at the thought that he was prepared to believe Lowenna. "Infact I don't think I want to see him again anyway!"

Marianne gave an impatient sigh. "I don't believe that for one moment. You two want your heads banged together. You're just as stubborn as him."

Naida smiled wryly. "I suppose so."

Having exhausted the topic of conversation, they sat silently eating their breakfast. Naida knew Marianne was exasperated with her attitude. But she couldn't humble herself to drop her pride.

She mulled over how Marianne had changed. It seemed to stem from the fire at the old church. She was inquisitive to know. Finally she made her confession.

"Remember the night of the fire?" she ventured slowly. "I was there."

Marianne glanced across at her, still remaining cool.

"I saw you," confirmed Naida. "I'm not condemning you. I realise you felt you had to do it and I'm glad you burnt that horrible tapestry."

There was no sign of remorse from Marianne. A closed expression hid any reaction. She sighed deeply and then opened her mouth to speak...

"It was me!"

They both turned to see Lowenna in the doorway, head bowed.

"It was me," she repeated, "I set fire to the church. The night of the solstice," she went on in a monotone voice. "The coven had planned a ceremony. We had been preparing for months. I found Mother was to be..." she stopped, unable to say the words. "I couldn't go though with it."

"It's alright Lowenna, soothed Marianne. "It's over now." She turned to Naida. "Please say nothing of this. Lowenna realises she had got in too deep. Those evil people drew her in like a fly to a spider's web."

Naida swallowed. "What did they intend to do?"

"You wouldn't want to know." Marianne clenched her fists together on the table. "No, you wouldn't want to know what went on in that church."

"Maybe you're right," said Naida jaggedly. She failed to comprehend how placid Marianne was being about it. Sudden anger made her rise up. "But how can you forgive her? Can you forget how ill they made you?"

"She is my daughter," replied Marianne calmly. "I love her but I'll not forget. We are all entitled to make one mistake in our lifetime. I have forgiven her."

Naida looked at Marianne and tried to understand how she could and more importantly, if she should. Then she turned her attention to Lowenna to see if she showed any genuine remorse. The girl appeared very subdued. Whether it was repentance or not was hard to tell.

"I shall find it hard to forgive her," Naida said icily. Suddenly she had to get out of there. She couldn't listen any more to Marianne's complacency and Lowenna's pathetic explanations. She needed some fresh air. Without a word she made for the door. Out she marched, through the farm and on to where the fields beckoned.

Naida walked for a long time, not sure where she was going. She felt like Aphrodite carried on the breath of Zephyrus, the west wind. Deep in the heart of the wood she came to a wide girthed Yew tree, gnarled and weather ravaged. She reached out and touched the beautiful bark. It was as if she was greeted by Horae, the Goddess of the seasons. She leaned against the trunk, and then sat down in the hollow between its great raised roots.

How long she sat there meditating she had no idea. Only when hunger called did she stir and become aware of her immediate surroundings again. For a moment she was disorientated and unsure of the way back. If she walked towards the sound of the sea, she knew she would eventually find the main road. The forest was still and shaded. She got up and looked to the sun glinting through the trees and strained her ears to catch the sea-wind.

Instead the afternoon air was filled with the tinkling sounds of a flute. Naida turned towards the music. Between some trees a shaft of sunlight straight from its source appeared to hold the form of a small boy. He stopped his tune for a second and nodded a cheeky grin at Naida. He then beckoned for her to follow him. She could hear the sound of the sea breeze coming from the opposite direction and was torn as to which way to go.

Her rational mind won. It would be foolish to go back into the wood in the hope that she would find the farm. It seemed practical to make for the road. When she looked back, the boy had vanished.

After awhile she began to fret about her logic. The forest became dense and she had to force her way through thickets, avoiding the stinging nettles. Eventually the trees thinned near to the main road leading to the sea. Her sigh of relief was stifled at the unexpected sight of her Stepfathers car parked on the verge.

Naida darted towards the nearest tree. But it was too late. He had seen her. He had the car door open in a flash and made quick progress across the clearing. Petros was not far behind.

"We've got her this time," Andreas shouted over his shoulder to Petros. "You get behind that clump of trees – we'll corner her."

Naida stood still behind her refuge and waited. The men had apparently thought she had escaped into the wood. When she thought the coast was clear she sprang out and sprinted towards the clump of trees and safety, straight into the trap.

"Got you!" Petros gripped her arms securely. "That was a stroke of luck. We were just planning on how to capture you."

"Yes," snarled Andreas," The Gods must have guided you here." He took her chin and lifted it. "You have given us a lot of trouble. We have had to evade the police all day. Now you will pay for it. We shall fly to Cyprus. Rico has returned already. We must contact him immediately."

Naida struggled against Petros's hold. "You cannot – I will not," she spat. "I am not your daughter – its abduction."

"If you are not my daughter, then I have been deceived all these years." Andreas face was purple with anger. "Someone must pay for this. Nobody does this to me and goes unpunished."

Naida's outrage matched his anger. "If you weren't such an egoist, my Mother would have told you. Mother's dead now – you made her life a misery. I think she paid the price in full. Can't you let her rest in peace?"

"Come – we go now," Andreas stormed and took hold of her ankles. The two men carried her across to their car and bundled her in.

As they sped off, Naida scanned the streets for a familiar face to come to her aid. She sent a last resort prayer to the complex Goddess Aphrodite.

Halfway down the road, Andreas turned to Petros. "We are running low on petrol. I thought you filled the tank up last night?"

"No," replied Petros. "You said you'd do it in the morning."

Here followed a torrent of displeasure by Andreas in his native tongue, which caused Naida to cover her ears. She shut her eyes to block out the sight of them. Then a thought struck her and she opened them quickly.

"There's a petrol station next turning on the left." She offered the information almost amicably.

"Good." Andreas turned briefly to glance at her. "That is obliging of you Naida. I hope you can see sense now." He gave her a sardonic smile. "No woman can resist the temptation of a rich man. It has its advantages – no?"

"Don't miss the turning." Naida gritted her teeth. If Andreas thought she would even consider participating in this conversation, he was deluded. She sat back in silent contempt and waited.

Andreas pulled in alongside the petrol pumps. Once the tank was filled he went to pay. Naida fidgeted and wondered how to get rid of Petros.

"I'm thirsty Petros," she said and swallowed, emphasizing the point. "Will you go and buy us all a drink for the journey?"

"No worries," he replied, then opened the dashboard and took out a bottle of water. "Here – there's plenty."

Naida took the bottle from him and felt like screaming.

Then he said, "However, I'm out of cigarettes – won't be long."

Whether the Goddess has answered her prayer or Petros was just plain stupid, Naida didn't stop to analyse. She was out of that car and running. Back within the comparative safety of the woods, she slowed down. She had a vague idea of the direction to take back to the farm.

Nevertheless, after a while she began to wonder if she was taking the correct route. She wandered on aimlessly. The sound of a twig made her jump. She looked round to see a squirrel darting away and sighed. The whole day had been a nightmare from the moment she had got up and it wasn't even Friday the thirteenth! Where was the little flute player when she needed him?

Then she saw the huge tree near to where the shaft of sunlight had been. But there was no sign of the flautist to guide her home. However, this time she followed the trail he had beckoned her down. To her surprise it wasn't long before she recognised where she was, on familiar ground. The first thing to do was contact the police. Andreas and Petros would be spitting fire by now and would be capable of anything.

Up a winding lane by a bunch of cottages, stood a red telephone box. It was a welcome sight. Post-haste she made a call to Sergeant Eames and explained the situation.

"I'll send out George now," came the Sergeants reply.

"Not on his own!" Naida stressed frantically. "He's no match for the two of them. He'll need backup. You'll have to hurry."

"You can count on us," replied Sergeant Eames. "We've already been to Old Moorstone Farm to question everyone. You should have stayed in. Now get yourself back to the Tregartha's and lock the doors."

Naida assured him she would and hung up. The remainder of the walk across the fields seemed to go on forever. The stretch of open land made her nervous. She felt exposed and vulnerable. Every noise and shadow caused her to jump. The last hundred yards, she ran, reached the door, went inside and bolted it.

Chapter 23

"I've taken Lowenna back to school. It appears she's been seeing this Petros behind our backs and passing on information about Naida," Ivor informed them over dinner. He turned to Naida. "I made her tell the police everything."

"I knew it," gasped Naida. "I suspected the two of them had got together." She thought of that day at Seal Island and their intended meeting at the village tea shop, when Petros had conveniently appeared.

"She admitted writing poison pen letters to Howard and told of Petros's involvement with the looters," continued Ivor, then added with wry amusement, "I don't think our local village police in have had so much excitement before. They intend to pull all the stops out in order to catch these two."

"So that's what she did." Naida clenched her teeth and considered how anyone could be so vindictive.

"Naida, I know it's asking a lot," said Ivor, "but if you agree not to press charges the police will not pursue the matter of the poison pen letters. All this has given Lowenna a fright. I don't think she will misbehave again. She's going to write and apologise to you."

Naida was curious that no one had mentioned the fire. Obviously they had not connected it with Lowenna. She glanced around the table and

251

concluded it was not up to her to inform them. Perhaps it would forever go unsolved.

"I won't press charges," she promised. "But I hope she has learned her lesson."

"You can be sure of that," affirmed Marianne. "Having to return to boarding school during the summer holidays will mean being under the head mistresses wing – and I can assure you she won't enjoy that at all. The thought of it happening again will be enough to reform her. You wait and see. I know my Lowenna."

Maybe she did, thought Naida acidly. She couldn't help feeling cynical. It didn't alter the fact that Lowenna had done her utmost to ruin her relationship with Howard and to all accounts, succeeded.

The next day the police arrived to take a statement from Naida. She was told by Sergeant Eames that if she required protection, George would stay at the farm. This she declined. Andreas and Petros wouldn't dare to show their faces.

By the end of the week the police had not made much progress and Naida was beginning to get restless. It was feasible, she reasoned, that her stepfather and brother were long gone. Any rational villain would be miles away by now. They had the option of sanctuary in Cyprus.

She longed to take a walk through the fields, into the wood and down to the sea. The sensation of sand between her toes became almost an obsession. Lightly, she walked across the kitchen tiles in her bare feet.

Marianne was engrossed in a book in the sitting room. Ivor was down at the smallholding, busy packing the home deliveries. Naida hesitated by the back door. Then, taking a deep breath, she opened it and walked out.

Briskly she strode across the farm and proceeded on into the open fields. An overwhelming sense of freedom exhilarated her. She felt like a bird set free from its cage. As she came to the edge of the wood, she stopped and watched the rays of the sun dance in and out of the leaves. It was enchanting. The wood was magical.

She decided she would find the ancient tree, sit within its roots and gain wisdom and strength from its forces. However, she could not retrace her route and settled for a fairly large oak. She sat beneath its shaded boughs and thought of Howard. It was here they should have met Midsummer Eve. She wondered what he had in mind when he said they were to frolic in the forest. Fantasizing about the uninhibited pleasures they would have had, she suddenly felt cheated and very sad.

Without him, the wood now seemed empty. She got up and ran through the bracken, snagging her long skirt in her haste. The flimsy Indian cotton tore easily into strips. A prisoner to her emotions, she had to get out of the wood and into the light.

The main road leading to the beach was crowded with holidaymakers. She had not bargained for this. All she desired was a quiet shoreline where she could sit and watch the waves roll in and out – listen to the hum of the sea and the sound of the seals. Gunwalloe was where she wanted to be.

It was an impulse thing to do but she had been in a strange mood all morning. She jumped on a bus heading for Church Cove. The seals were settled in their usual place. Naida climbed down the cliff and joined them. A boat was secured nearby and Naida assumed it was Blake's. Howard would have left him in charge.

She relaxed in the secluded bay, enjoying the tranquillity. The seals welcomed the company, hooting and showing off in the shallows. Naida had taken for granted the boat was vacant. However, without warning the cabin door shot open. To her horror, Petros stepped out and stretched his stocky form.

The seclusion of the bay suddenly became claustrophobic. Naida froze. There was no way she could reach the top of the cliff before they spotted her. She tried to duck down behind the seals. The movement caught Petros' attention.

"Father," he called. "Look what we have here."

A dishevelled Andreas appeared from the cabin. "Aha!" he jeered. "Didn't we always call her the little fish? What did I tell you! I knew sooner or later we would make our catch by the sea."

Naida stood up and raced towards the cliff. She knew she hadn't a chance. Before she had taken a few steps up the cliff path, Petros was behind her, dragging her down by her ankles. She fell in an ungainly heap onto the sand. He pulled her up like a rag doll and flung her unceremoniously over his shoulder.

Andreas waited in the boat while his son hauled in their prey. "Put her down below and tie her wrists

– we don't want any more mistakes," he said, as if she was no more than a prize to be bargained with.

Petros opened the hatch and was about to drop her down the stairs.

"Treat her with kid gloves. She's worth a mint to us," sneered Andreas. "Our precious treasure will lose its value if it's damaged."

"You'll not get away with this!" stormed Naida. But how she was going to escape this time evaded her. If only she hadn't been so stupid. She had underestimated just how cunning her Stepfather could be. There was no way he would ever let her go.

"It's planned down to the last detail," replied Andreas, "I have a flight booked to Cyprus. All we have to do is get to the airport and one extra passenger will be a bonus." He started the boat and discreetly they drifted out to sea.

Down below in the cabin, Naida sat in a state of shock. She struggled to free her bound wrists. It all appeared hopeless. Perhaps when they got to the airport, she could alert someone for help. Yes – that would be her best bet, she reasoned.

She could hear Andreas and Petros moving about on the deck. Looking up she noticed the hatch had no lock on it. Her wrists were now free. Noiselessly, she climbed the stairs and poked her head out. The men had their backs to her, navigating their route; she slipped out silently and crept round to the other side. Crouching behind a box, she surveyed their position. They appeared to be heading out into the open sea, but where?

"We've plenty of time to reach the airport," Andreas was saying to Petros. "She saved us a lot of trouble, turning up like that. We might have had to leave without her."

Petros grinned at his Father. "I was looking forward to breaking into that farmhouse and stealing her from under their noses."

"You're too reckless Petros. You have to use your head," rebuked Andreas. "It will be your downfall."

"We are only taking what is rightly ours," stated Petros.

"That is so," agreed Andreas. "But we have to be clever. The law is on her side. If we can get to Cyprus, no one can touch us."

Naida gasped with astonishment. If they had carried out their original plan, the Tregartha's would have once again been dragged into this mess. What was she to do? Frantically she looked about her. Please let another boat come by, she prayed.

Sail ships bobbed up and down in the distance, too far away to see them. From that direction a whirring sound, like a hive of bees, began to grow louder. Then she saw a speed boat emerge from the centre of the colourful sails. Andreas increased their speed and attempted to swerve away from the oncoming boat.

Naida saw the police uniform on the deck and jumped up, elated.

"Help! Help!" she screamed, waving her arms wildly.

"Get her back down below," bellowed Andreas as he struggled with the wheel.

256

The boat was rocking out of control in the swell. Naida ran to the rear and continued to wave.

"I can't steady her," shrieked Andreas, "grab the wheel."

The police boat was within shouting range now. Naida could see the stern Sergeant on board with George, who seemed to be enjoying every minute.

Andreas and Petros battled with the boat and managed to steer towards dry land. Naida watched in dismay as the other boat fell back away from them. Clumsily, Andreas came to ground.

"Quick – grab her and make for the car," he yelled as he hurriedly snatched their suitcase and jumped out.

Naida clung to the stern for as long as she could. The police boat was rapidly gaining on them. However, Petros wrenched her free and dragged her, protesting, to their waiting car.

As they sped away she glimpsed the irate Sergeant coming in to ground. All she hoped for was that they had seen them disappearing off in the car.

"We did it – we've lost them," Petros broke into raucous shrieks of laughter.

"Don't relax yet," replied the more cautious Andreas. "We've still got to get to the airport."

"You've got to admit – that was some chase." Petros' expression was wild. He thrived on the excitement of living on the edge.

Naida looked out of the back window in the hope of being followed. She strained to listen for the sound of the police sirens in pursuit. None was forthcoming and she sank down in her seat defeated.

When they reached the airport, Naida had to admit there was little chance of anyone coming to her rescue. They had won. Andreas parked the car, and then opened his suitcase. He took out three passports and plane tickets. He obviously had been well prepared.

"Keep these safe," he ordered, handing them to Petros.

Petros put them to his lips and kissed them mockingly. "Ah," he said. "Passport to a life of luxury."

Andreas glanced around furtively. He gestured for Naida to get out of the car, and then locked the doors. While the two men checked the passports, Naida took the opportunity to go on ahead in the hope of losing them.

"Wait!" demanded Andreas, "Don't be foolish."

Petros caught up with her and escorted her inside. He was determined she would not do anything to cancel his chance of a fortune.

Wedged between the two men at the check-in, Naida was counting on someone becoming suspicious. Her eyes beseeched the other travellers, but to no avail. All seemed uninterested or unaware of her plight.

The check-in girl smiled as she greeted them and looked over their tickets. Naida gave her an anxious stare. But no – politely the girl wished them a good journey and handed back their tickets. Naida began to panic. As a last resort, she was forced to make a scene.

In a loud voice she said. "I want you to call the police. These men are abducting me against my will."

The check-in girl looked flustered. Andreas and Petros took hold of Naida's arms.

Andreas smiled condescendingly. "Come now my dear. You know what the doctor said. You mustn't get upset." He turned to the onlookers apologetically. "She's just come out of hospital. We are taking her on holiday to convalesce."

The crowd looked on in a mixture of amazement and curiosity.

"It's not true," shouted Naida. "You must believe me." In her desperation she wondered how people could be so indifferent.

"It's a mental illness," explained Andreas and forced her away towards departures.

Appalled at her predicament, she sat on the plane in a state of complete shock. Andreas drummed his fingers on the arm rest, impatient for the plane to take off.

"Why is it taking so long?" he whispered nervously to Petros.

"Lighten up Father – it will take off shortly. We'll soon be on our way." Petros relaxed in the window seat, pleased with their progress. He reclined the back rest. "Mission accomplished."

"Sorry for the delay." The pilot's voice came over the intercom. There's a slight hitch. Please remain in your seats."

Andreas looked around in alarm. "What the hell's going on?"

"Take it easy," said Petros, "it's probably a late passenger. It's quite common."

The respite gave Naida a chance to gather her wits about her. She looked around and couldn't believe her eyes. Sergeant Eames and George were walking steadily up the aisle. She wanted to jump for joy and kiss her knights in shining armour. In a daze she heard the Sergeant speak.

He stood before Petros. "I'm arresting you for attempted murder, blackmail, looting and abduction." He turned to Andreas. "And you for accessory to the fact."

Naida heard the clink of handcuffs and watched in a trance like state as the men were led away. As they went, shouting their protestations, it was all too much for her and she fainted. Infact she was not aware of the fuss she caused. In the ambulance that sped her back, she drifted in and out of consciousness.

Chapter 24

The next thing Naida knew, she was waking up in her bedroom at Old Moorstone Farm. Voices were talking softly as if from a long way off.

"She's opened her eyes, thank goodness," said Marianne.

As Naida came to, she recognised Marianne's face swimming in front of her. Ivor stood behind with a look of concern.

"You had us worried," he said

"My Stepfather!" exclaimed Naida as it all came rushing back. "Andreas and Petros – what happened?"

"Don't worry – they are being held at the police station," soothed Marianne. "You're safe now. It seems you collapsed with the stress of it all."

It was as if a great weight had been lifted from Naida's shoulders. She could hardly believe it was over. The only thing that marred her happiness was the fact that Howard wasn't here to give her his support. Her heart sank.

"Sergeant Eames wants to talk to you," said Ivor. "But not now – when you're up to it," he smiled gently. "How do you feel?"

"Starving!" declared Naida. "I haven't eaten since breakfast."

"No wonder you fainted," empathised Marianne. "Ivor," she said, turning to her husband. "Ask Mrs Dunn to bring up some food for Naida please."

"I'll get it myself," he grinned. "I want to see some colour in those cheeks."

261

When he had gone, Marianne brought over the dressing table stool and sat beside the bed. "It was naughty of you to go off like that this morning." Her concern for Naida caused her to scold her. "You were told to stay close to the house."

"Sorry," answered Naida meekly. She looked down at her hands clasped together on the bed.

Marianne softened. "At least those men have been caught."

"Yes." Naida glanced up positively. "We may have lived in fear for weeks if I hadn't gone for that walk."

"That's no excuse," replied Marianne soberly.

Naida sighed, "You're right." They sat for a while in silence. Naida was in deep thought. Finally she looked at Marianne and said, "Lowenna's explanations were pathetic. How can you…?"

"Lowenna isn't well," cut in Marianne, "She's going to need counselling and I really do appreciate that you kept silent about the fire."

"I wonder whether I did the right thing," Naida agonised over her decision. It disturbed her to think of the misery Lowenna had caused.

"It's over and done with," said Marianne with finality. "We must pray for her."

Naida lay back on the pillow. Marianne's tone had made it clear that the subject was closed. The only consolation was the knowledge that Lowenna was not her blood sister.

"I had a half brother, didn't I?" she asked, and then lowered her eyes. Perhaps she was being tactless.

"Yes," whispered Marianne. "How did you know?"

"Mrs Dunn – she said he was musical. Did he play an instrument?"

"Why yes," Marianne brightened proudly. "He played a flute."

Naida's jaw dropped. She sat up, alert. It all fell into place - the little boy in the woods – the sound of the flute in the hall and in her dreams. Her spirit brother was looking after her. She was eager to tell Marianne. Then again, it was perhaps best kept as her secret. Hers and Derwin's. She lay back down on the pillow with a look of contentment.

By the end of October, autumn had played her melancholy game scattering leaves across the land, dancing sombrely on the edge on the season, wiping the smile from the sun. Leaves turned shades of russet, orange and ochre. Although the Indian summer had prolonged the good weather, the holiday season was over. To Naida, it became increasingly obvious that Howard would not be returning. She realised that she had been romantically deluded and therefore resolved to come to terms with her future.

Tom, to everyone's relief had made a complete recovery. He was allowed home and had to take it easy. Naida often sat with him. Their conversations distracted her from her difficult decision. Howard was rarely far from her thoughts – his face haunted her. Life had lost its shape and direction. However it was time to move on – start afresh somewhere far away, with no memories of him.

Tom was sitting out the front in the comfortable chair, just as Naida had first seen him the day she arrived. She had the urge to rush over and hug him – make him beg her to stay. Instead she said, somewhat gravely, "Tom – I have something to tell you."

He motioned for her to join him.

"I've decided to go back to London. I need to concentrate on a career. It's the practical thing to do." She was trying to convince herself. It was the best choice for everyone concerned. Although she knew her heart would always be in Cornwall.

Tom's face fell. "My dear – you know how much you'll be missed. Are you sure about this?"

Naida suppressed her emotions and answered simply. "It is what I want now." She had only brought trouble and pain to this place – to these people she loved.

"You have to do what you think is best for you," he smiled. "You'll always be welcome 'ere. Will you go back to the house in London?"

"No," Naida shuddered, "I couldn't. I have friends who will put me up until I find a job and flat of my own."

Tom nodded. The silence between them was companionable. Finally he said, "Want to hear a tale about the upstream fish and the downstream fish?"

Naida looked at him sideways. "You'll tell me anyway."

"The upstream fish always make an effort," began Tom. "They fight against the current – seeking to be inspired – rising above the reeds that could entangle and drag 'em under in despair."

Naida understood what he was saying. She marvelled at this wise old man. "And what about the downstream fish?"

"Now 'im – he just goes with the flow thinks that everyone will arrive at where they're going sooner or later, so why bother to try?"

"That sounds defeatist," observed Naida.

Tom winked "Who is right? Think about it…"

Over dinner, Naida broke the news to Ivor and Marianne.

"It appears your mind is made up," said Ivor resignedly, "and I suppose there's nothing we can say to alter it."

"There's more chance of finding suitable work in London," she assured them. She was making an effort to be optimistic. "Of course I will come and visit next summer."

Her enthusiasm had not fooled them. Beneath her brightness they knew how betrayed she felt about Howard. Ivor had written to him and informed him of everything. He was disappointed in Howard for not replying.

"When will you be leaving?" asked Ivor.

"Tomorrow," Naida answered quickly.

"So soon?" said Marianne.

"I guess it's time to put my talents to the test," Naida said jovially, overriding her despondency.

"And I'm sure you'll be snapped up by any prospective employers," replied Ivor. He was determined to make her last evening at Old Moorstone Farm one to be remembered with happiness.

"You'll be an asset," agreed Marianne warmly. She too had picked up on the hurt Naida was feeling. How could Howard forget her so quickly?

Tom had gone down to the cellar and appeared with a bottle of their best wine. Over dinner, they spent a long time talking. The wine lightened any friction in the atmosphere and Tom told a tale or two of his adventures as a young fisherman.

"Many a tall tale!" Ivor winked at Naida and they all laughed.

By the time Naida went to bed, she was in a light hearted mood – almost forgetting her sadness. Tomorrow she would be miles away from Cornwall and her new found family. Pensively, she sat combing her hair at the dressing table. She sighed, got into bed and closed her eyes. She quickly drifted off. In her dreams Aphrodite was sitting on a rock, garlanded with flowers. She confronted Psyche with a task to perform. This she must do if she wants to win back Eros...

The following morning Naida awoke late and decided to take the overnight train to London. This gave her time to tie up loose ends and say her goodbyes in the village. Before she left, there was one place she wanted to take a last look. She had to say farewell to the seals at Gunwalloe, Church Cove; drawn there by the magic of the place that held a thousand memories.

A couple of late holidaymakers watched her walk down the cliff path. They appeared intrigued by her head turning exotic looks and wondered if perhaps she was descended from the invading Spanish who had arrived with the Armada.

The tide was out, enabling her to sit on the rock and enjoy the fresh, salty spray from the sea. I'm going to miss this; she thought and suddenly had the desire to be the downstream fish. Then she wouldn't have to go away at all. Life had left her disillusioned.

For a long time, early evening, she sat, just gazing into the distance. This place had got into her blood. She couldn't disguise her immense sensitivity out here alone. A tear rolled down her cheek. She closed her eyes and recalled the first time she had met Howard in such extraordinary circumstances. How he had scolded her. Obviously they were not meant to be together. She recalled something he had once said. It seemed a long time ago now -something about a legend. What was lt? Then she remembered his words: If a black haired maiden sits on yonder Croony rock... She sighed.

Squinting through her tears, she didn't see the ship coming over the horizon at first. She wiped her eyes, and then opened them wide. Something was noticeable in the distance. Was her mind doing the tricks again? No –it couldn't be! She didn't believe in miracles any more – even though it was the eve of Samhain the Pagan festival.

The evening star appeared to rise in the heavens. A feeling came over Naida of being at one with the universe – in her flow. The ship came clearly into view and a small boat was lowered to the side. Naida held her breath. This was unreal. Then the boat was drawing level and suddenly she was being held in Howard's strong arms.

"My mermaid," he whispered.

Naida felt elated and complete all at once. The Gods must be looking after her. "How did you know?"

"It must be predestined," he said with a wink. "Who are we to question? However, it was Ivor, your Father, who wrote to me. He managed to trace the ship I was on – he told me everything. My darling Naida – can you ever forgive me? I was such a fool to believe Lowenna." He cupped her face in his hands. "Please say you will marry me? Come live with me in our cottage down by the sea.

She had no need to think twice. She answered without hesitation. "Yes." She looked at him and knew it was their destiny to be together.

Like their ancestors before them, they belonged to the seas and all the creatures of the seas belonged to them. And no more than the eternal cycle of the cosmos could be separated from all the stars in existence, could they be freed from their fate.

"Oh yes," she repeated. Her hair blew softly with the breeze in the dying light of the evening. The sky met the cliffs behind them, all part of a single untameable entity.

"I never want to lose you again," he whispered as he held her against him. "I couldn't bear to be away from you for one minute."

"Never," she murmured.

"I'll have no need to venture on long fishing trips."

"We can work together to save the seals," said Naida, as the pleasant thought occurred to her.

"And you, my love, can paint to your hearts content. I'll build you a studio and you can exhibit at one of those galleries at St. Ives."

She sighed. How could anyone be this happy? She could walk through the woods again without fear. Safe in the knowledge that her little flute player would always be there to protect her.

In tune with her thoughts, Howard was also thinking of his beloved woods. He half closed his eyes and looked at her seductively.

"There will always be another Midsummer Solstice," he said. Then lifting her onto the boat, murmured, "I love you."

Her reply was silenced with a kiss.

"Right," he said purposefully. "I'm taking you home to bed, before I ravish you right here in this boat."

"Lucky I've already packed my case then," she smiled provocatively.

He raised an eyebrow. "So – you knew I was coming for you?"

"Not exactly – but I had a feeling," she said evasively. There would be plenty of time to explain.

"After we are married we shall fulfil Lilith's prophecy. The next generation will be a happy one." His lips curved in a sensuous smile. Her legs turned to jelly.

"That sounds good to me – I…" She closed her eyes as he planted another kiss on her parted lips.

Their spirits blended. Their life's vocation was about to begin.

Epilogue

She waited for him in the heart of the wood, sitting at the base of the stout yew tree, its roots embedded in the soil, gaining and giving nourishment. She raised her head to receive the light from the Spiritual sun, glinting through the Evergreen. It illumined the Celtic cross placed around her neck, reminding her of the gift of belonging.

He would be climbing the cliff path now, leaving behind his beloved seal sanctuary, the rush of the ocean ringing in his ears. He would pause to glance down the stern coastline. His eyes would wander over the sea-carved boulders, coated with yellow lichen and one in particular would fill him with reverence. Croony rock had altered the course of his fate as sure as she had willed it.

With newly awakened vision, Naida could see her children, yet unborn, weaving across the dappled woodland glade, playing in the sea – running free. This was the eve of the Midsummer Solstice, bringing with it the power of rebirth in nature for Mother Earth. Special blessings would concern the human family. Perhaps she would conceive tonight.

Attuned to the elements, she breathed in their strength. Howard, her husband, joined her, the music of his heartbeat in the atmosphere like sparkling wine. Now they would renew their vows with a Hand Fasting ceremony that would bind them together forever. She wore a long flowing gossamer gown; a circle of flowers adorned her hair. The sacred space was lit by candles and perfumed incense. A ring of rose petals was laid out around them. They stood facing each other akin to Eros and Psyche reunited in truthful love. As they gazed with love for each other, their wrists were bound together with a lovers knot. They jumped the broomstick. There was celebration and magical merriment. Behind them in the heavens, Aphrodite raised a golden cup to sanctify their union, for even the potency of unlimited love can influence the Gods.

3802131R00155

Printed in Great Britain
by Amazon.co.uk, Ltd.,
Marston Gate.